QUIET AS DEATH

Kelly knocked on the door. "Hello?" No answer. Just a creepy, eerie silence.

Feeling a chill, Kelly pushed on the door. It swung open and she stepped in. The living room lampstand had been knocked over and the cord had been torn out at the base. It was missing.

What was going on?

Kelly wandered down the hall toward the back bedroom.

"Hello? The door was open, and I . . ."

Kelly stopped talking. Stopped breathing.

It took a few minutes before she stopped screaming . . .

Other Avon Flare Books by
Robert Hawks

HALL PASS
SUMMER'S END

THE
SUBSTITUTE

ROBERT HAWKS

AN AVON  FLARE BOOK

THE SUBSTITUTE is an original publication of Avon Books. This work has never before appeared in book form. This work is a novel. Any similarity to actual persons or events is purely coincidental.

AVON BOOKS
A division of
The Hearst Corporation
1350 Avenue of the Americas
New York, New York 10019

Copyright © 1995 by Robert Hawks
Published by arrangement with the author
Library of Congress Catalog Card Number: 95-90104
ISBN: 0-380-77622-7
RL: 5.9

First Avon Flare Printing: October 1995

AVON FLARE TRADEMARK REG. U.S. PAT. OFF. AND IN OTHER COUNTRIES, MARCA REGISTRADA, HECHO EN U.S.A.

Printed in the U.S.A.

RA   10   9   8   7   6   5   4   3   2   1

The very emphasis of the commandment: Thou shalt not kill, makes it certain that we are descended from an endlessly long chain of generations of murderers, whose love of murder was in their blood as it is perhaps also in ours.

—SIGMUND FREUD

THE SUBSTITUTE

OPERATION TORMENT

"Protect The Ones You Love!"

1. Detect Evil
2. Understand Evil
3. *Destroy* Evil

Kelly Wallis's world used to end all the time, but
having always felt the occasional doomsday good
for building character, she never let it bring her
down. Tragedy begets bright sides; for every bad
thing the universe slung in your direction you were
inevitably offered back a gift. If you waited for it,
stayed patient, kept your eyes open. Good came
from bad, or at least always had so far.

Example: Kelly's mom and dad divorced when
she was eleven, but Ma wound up with a new job
and moved from Chicago to Long Beach, Indiana,
so Kelly and her mother got out of the city. Good
from bad. Kelly flunked seventh grade algebra, but
on retaking it the next year met the MoKid—Melissa Kidder—who became her best friend. Good
from bad. Kelly nearly died in a car accident, and
her Ma met the man of her dreams.

Good from bad.

Sort of.

It was true, though, that the first time she met
her stepfather-to-be he was pleased to find Kelly
alive, and very determined to keep her that way.
She was in a horrible car accident, and he was the

one who found her pinned inside the overturned vehicle, on a sloping concrete embankment, ready to slide down and into the icy river. This when Kelly was fourteen, on a lousy day in February. Riding in the front seat with her cousin Rocky—Linda Rockowski, who was driving—Kelly never actually realized what was happening until it was over; the whole skid was a sudden shimmering, shuddering blur. The road became snow, which became ice, which became glass, and they sailed through the guardrail like it was butter, and into space.

Kelly felt that stomach drop, that falling sensation, but it seemed more as if the earth below was crashing up, spinning and racing toward them louder than a thousand earthquakes or a million thunderstorms. Later the cops said the car rolled five times, but Kelly wasn't counting. Not then; all she knew then was a thud of quiet.

Nothingness.

Black. Except it wasn't really black, it was still that shimmering blue, and she felt nauseous, like she might throw up.

Or *down.* Kelly was upside-down, she realized then; her center of gravity in the wrong place, her weight pushing against the straps of the seat belt, but something heavy and firm held her lower body still while she hung there. *Hung where?*

Dead? Trapped? Pinned? Twisting her head—which ached, everything ached—Kelly saw Rocky beside her; she was unconscious, her eyelids fluttering. Kelly tried to talk to her, but managed only a whisper. "Rocky . . . hey, *Rocky. . . .*"

Then sounds came back. The creaking of sagging metal, the crunching of the car roof. The smell of gas was everywhere, and the door beside her impossibly mangled; she couldn't open it, couldn't budge herself, was hanging upside down hurting all over, especially her right leg, the knee and below. Snow was settling on and around them, then would stop, only to come again when the creaking car jiggled or the wind shifted.

Kelly choked, then lost control and started crying; she kept wondering how much it was going to hurt when the car slipped, tilted, and slid down the embankment. The car would roll some more, probably crushing itself flat, with her in it.

Us in it, she told herself. *Us.* Cousin Rocky was going to be okay, wasn't she? *Wasn't she?* Except how was she going to be okay if they were both going to die? Thinking made no sense.

Lights came soon after that; who knew how long afterward? Strobe lights, red-and-blue flashes which reached even down where they were. A big yellow-haired man in a blue uniform, crawling on his belly down beside the crunched car, he seemed pleasantly surprised to find Kelly alive. "Hey, hey, honey, how you doing in there?"

Kelly was sure she made sounds, nothing beyond that. It was a tight, terrifying place; things were creaking, popping now. She wasn't breathing right, just in gasps.

"Easy, *easy*," the yellow-haired man said, trying to pull open the car door. No use. "Hang on there, I've got to go get something."

Not wanting him to leave her, Kelly tried to say,

3

"No, wait . . ." Except he was already gone.

Only for a few minutes, though. When he came back, with tools, he started working on the door with something, talking as he did. The flashlight he carried occasionally illuminated his face. "The lottery numbers are out. Did you take 6-24-26-53 and 19?"

Kelly said nothing. Lowering his voice, the yellow-haired guy said, "Hey, you know, I gotta tell you. We have got to stop meeting like this— my girlfriend is starting to be suspicious."

Above there was a heavy creak and rumble; the car was shifting and snow blew all around, settling on his face. It was coming down now, Kelly knew it, and she felt like whimpering, maybe even started, but realized if the car slid it was going to slide right over the yellow-haired guy. Her own fear choked on the fact that he was being so brave, so . . . casual. Making jokes.

The yellow-haired guy smiled again. "Don't worry about that, that's just the wind, I think. My name's Doug, and you'll know when it gets dangerous because Doug will be away from here screaming like a banshee. I am a total capital letter C *Coward*. . . ."

He handed her a foil wrap, a thick silver blanket. Stuffing it in through the shattered window, in to Kelly, saying as he did, "Now allow me to introduce you to the latest in fashion accessories. Can't buy this in stores, you know. I'm going to cut through the door with a small torch, and sometimes I screw up and accidentally cut right through the

4

person—just kidding. See if you can push it around your legs. Great.''

He lit the flame now, and it sparked but she couldn't see, just something cutting. Snow was blowing inside the car; she saw flakes settling on Rocky's face by the flickering light. Close to panic, Kelly trembled as this Doug guy kept talking to her.

"So, anyway, what kind of car is this? A BMW? German car? I drive this really cheap thing that has all the resale value of a box of used Kleenex. Then again, so does this BMW now, I guess. *Just kidding.* . . .''

He was finished cutting. Sweat covered his face, or maybe it was melting snow, and his eyes were a deep brown. He was beautiful. He was saving her life.

Swallowing now, Kelly even talked. "I think my leg is broken or something.''

Working on prying the door open, he considered this and said, "Well, I have to be honest. If I get you out of here and catch you complaining about a sore leg, missy, I may just punch you in the nose.''

A few strong motions later and he got the door open in pieces. Keeping her inside the foil blanket, he dragged her out of the vehicle, grunting, using all his strength to pull and talk Kelly out of there. "Normally,'' he said, "normally we have stretchers and paramedics and all that nifty stuff like on TV, but to be honest, well, nobody else wanted to get their uniforms dirty. Me, I get off in an hour so it don't matter. Come on, a little faster, we gotta

5

make my boss think this was scary . . .''

Sky. He got her out under the sky then, under the bright stars, *safe*, and they were pounced on by people. She went into an ambulance, and he crawled back down to the car and got her cousin Rocky, who, it turned out, was only unconscious and survived even better than Kelly did. Kelly's right leg was never the same, the bone broken in two places, the knee shot; she wound up in a brace for almost a year. Rocky was pretty much okay.

Ten minutes or so later the car slipped again before they could get a tow truck hooked up to it, and it slid into the river. If they'd still been inside they would have (a) frozen, (b) drowned, and (c) there is no (d).

Doug's full name turned out to be Doug Wozniak. He came by the hospital later, on his own time, just to see if Kelly and her cousin were all right, and that's where he met Ma; Kelly always supposed she was still in shock, just grateful for her daughter's life.

Then again, though, Doug was a blond, brown-eyed hero, definitely the type; probably Ma really fell for him. They started going out on dates, and four months later he moved in, and a month after that it turned out they were married. No ceremony, no celebration, just an announcement at breakfast.

Which was important, Kelly always thought later, because it was almost a month after that before she saw him hit her for the first time. . . .

Which isn't to say he hadn't done it before; probably he had. Ma had bruises, accidents, but it

6

never occurred to Kelly that Doug the thug was doing it, not until the cheeseburger thing, and even then she knew to approach it from the bright side. Good from bad.

Ma was a strong, pretty lady, but when Kelly got home from school on Cheeseburger Day Ma was cowering, her right eye was going black, bruising. Without even thinking Kelly said, "Oh my God."

"It's okay."

"Ma."

"It's okay, Kelly."

"It's not okay."

Doug ambled back into the kitchen.

Ma settled back against the refrigerator.

"Cheeseburgers," said Doug.

Cheeseburgers. Well, Kelly thought, that explains everything. *Or nothing, one of the two.*

"How hard can it be to cook up a stupid cheeseburger?"

"I'm sorry." This from Ma.

He backed off some, and she stole back what space she could. Kelly felt like screaming, but wanted Ma to do it first. *Come on.* Ma never did anything selfish, she always had something better in mind. Some things had been knocked over on the counter, and she started rearranging the knick-knacks, salt and pepper shakers mostly. She placed them in neat little rows.

Ma was tired. Getting older by the day.

Scream. Come on and scream.

Why didn't she just throw him out? Kelly wondered.

Doug was pacing. Not unusual. Usually it

7

seemed as if he was pacing. He took a second to snap off Ma's CD player, the one Kelly bought her for the kitchen. He was always insulting her music. "No wonder you can't pay attention to your cooking, what with this crap eating at your eardrums."

"It grows on you."

"Fungus grows on you. And then there's this crap." He grabbed the pile of *Impossible Detective* magazines from the counter and flung them at the trash bucket; some went in, most banged off and onto the floor. "I don't even like that stuff around. I see enough gore at work, I have to come home to it, too?"

"I'm sorry. . . ."

"Look, I didn't just fall off of a banana boat. I'm out there busting my butt every day, I risk my life out there every day, and when I get home I don't ask for much. A beer, some TV, maybe something good to eat."

"I know."

Grabbing at the plate, he held up a crunched, battered burger, suddenly throwing it at Ma. "Does this look done to you? The meat's red. I ain't no animal. I kind of sort of like my food cooked, you know? Would it kill you to toss this thing on the grill a few seconds before you shove it at me?"

"I'm sorry."

"This the kind of cheeseburger your old man would eat?"

Ma's old man, Kelly's grandfather.

"I don't know," she said.

"Well, don't start with that crap again. Daddy's gone. I'm your daddy now."

8

No answer from Ma. No look, either. Hardly any breathing.

"What? You can't look me in the face now?"

Kelly tried to speak:

"Ma . . ."

"You stay out of this, Knock-Knock." Knock-Knock was what Ma called Kelly sometimes, a holdover nickname from when Kelly had an affection for knock-knock jokes, every old knock-knock joke in history. Doug glared at Kelly. "You owe me."

As always. He would never, ever let Kelly forget how he saved her life. He was starting to rant, but the phone started ringing and Kelly answered it. It was the police station, Captain Morris; he knew and liked Kelly; they both took on the world smiling. "Hey, Knock-Knock, how are you?"

"Fine, sir."

"Sorry to bother, but I need to talk to the sarge for a minute."

Sergeant Wozniak, Long Beach Metropolitan Police Department.

"Only a minute?"

"Just a minute."

"Okay, hang on," Kelly said, interrupting the kitchen scene, looking at Doug with nothing but contempt. Then she offered over the phone. "Ma? It's for you, Ma. . . ."

From *Impossible Detective* magazine, June issue, page 178, classified section, Investigative Column:

AURORA, IL: Bank teller called Robbins, AKA Harry Newsome, Harry Fent, Harry Whatley, 6'1", 210lbs, WM Appx 30–35, sometimes uses English accent, hangouts yuppie bars, art cinemas, last seen op yellow sports car, UNKWN make—reward! Contact Detect #246-99-0885.

Kelly's mother, Detective Sergeant Patricia Wallis-Wozniak, was the first hero she ever had, teaching her always to search for a bright and shiny side of things, and she was even famous for a while, not for shooting somebody, but because of somebody she didn't shoot.

Kelly wasn't there, but she knew the story as well as anyone. Ma was out with her partner Greg, and they stopped at a 7-Eleven for something. Greg waited with the car; Ma was inside getting a soda or something. Suddenly there was an outburst at the front of the store. A woman clerk was screaming, and a robber was shouting at her in wild Spanish as he waved a gun.

Lots of cops would have come out blazing then. Wanted to shoot, enjoyed doing it. Not Kelly's mother.

Ma pushed herself back into a rack of potato chips and pulled her .38 out; never before had she pulled her gun at work. She was totally calm. The terrified clerk was stuffing money from the register into a plastic grocery bag as the robber continued to wildly wave his gun.

Ma waited. Took a couple of breaths. She wanted the robber to back away from the counter, stop waving his gun at the woman behind the counter. Finally he did move, turning to make his escape, and Ma leapt out into the aisle, drawing down and screaming in Spanish—which she spoke fluently—"Freeze! Don't move!"

The robber spun, gun aimed. Ma tensed but didn't shoot. Neither did the robber. The woman clerk was crying, and Ma talked to both of them, the clerk in English, the robber in Spanish, all the while standing there in classic combat position, knees bent, her .38 aimed at the chest of the guy with the gun.

"Get down behind the counter," she told the crying girl. "You'll be all right, get down."

Then to the robber, in Spanish again: "Easy, brother. Nobody wants to die today."

"I'll kill you."

"Maybe. Maybe you don't shoot so good as I do. I get paid to practice, you know. I go to the pistol range two, maybe three times a month. They pay me to go. I could split a melon from ten times this distance, a melon the size of your head. How good a shot are you?"

The robber was trembling, scared. He wanted to quit, but didn't know how. He was scared. "Even if I give up you'll still kill me. I hear about that all the time."

"No way," said Ma. "Too much paperwork."

The robber was weeping now, crying. "If . . . If I give my gun and give back the money, can I go

12

home? Please? I'm sorry, I'm sorry. I don't feel good.''

Ma didn't say anything, she just slowly shook her head. Still crying, the robber set his gun down on the floor, along with the money. Ma eased herself forward and took up his gun. The robber was bawling like a baby, and he didn't give any more trouble.

What made Ma a hero, though, was this. The robber guy wasn't a drug addict, or a thug; he had a baby sister who needed a kidney transplant, but there was no money, no way to pay for the operation. The guy was under a lot of pressure, hadn't slept for days, and just cracked from desperation. And the one person who needed him most in the world was just an innocent little nine-year-old girl, and when the publicity started all of the sudden the money appeared for her, of course, but there was only one suitable donor—her big brother. If Ma had shot him dead in the store, she would have also been shooting that little girl.

So Kelly's mother was a hero.

They talked about it only one time, because Kelly wanted Ma to know how impressed she was, just like everybody else. This was before the accident, before Doug the thug fireman, before the stepfather, when it was just the two of them, Patty and Kelly. Ma was getting all these commendations, from the mayor, the governor, local leaders, etc. Everybody was saying how it showed police officers could resolve situations without coming in blasting, how a good police officer can control a situation so that violence doesn't have to be part of the equation.

Of course Kelly didn't understand it that way. She just knew Ma had busted up a robbery, nobody got hurt, and she was a little bit famous.

Ma sat her on the couch, wanting to put all that out of her thoughts; Ma was a little hesitant. "Kelly, you don't understand."

"Understand what?"

"I . . . I'm no hero. I keep trying to keep this in perspective, look at the bright side, but I was about two seconds from blowing that guy's head off." Ma was smoking again, and she lit another cigarette.

This set Kelly back in her chair, thinking about it. "Yeah, but . . . you waited. Isn't that the bright side? Isn't it good to wait?"

"Not always. . . ." Ma had given it all a lot of thought, and she still wasn't sure she had done the right thing. "I keep picturing him spinning around, except now he shoots, he shoots and I take a bullet in my face because I didn't react fast enough, because I didn't fire."

"But you were right."

"I was lucky."

Kelly didn't know what to say to that.

Ma stubbed out her cigarette, Kelly noticing for the first time—ever—that her mother's hands were trembling. "I won't ever wait again," she said, getting up. "From now on I'm going to be Bang-Bang Patty. . . ."

Fair enough, thought Kelly then and now, although her mother had yet to face a similar situ-

14

ation. They'd made an interesting pair, Bang-Bang Patty and Knock-Knock Kelly. Bang-Bang and Knock-Knock. Sounded like a couple of characters off of the "Flintstones."

It was shortly after that Ma started to bring home *Impossible Detective* magazine. . . .

Sixteen years old with shoulder-length brown hair, Kelly considered herself an interventionist, a person who did things rather than waiting to see others do them first. She was also a bright student at school; why not? Usually paying attention in class was easier than giving in to distractions, numerous as they might be.

Besides, Kelly got along really well with just about everybody, including her teachers, and especially Mrs. Hanson, her American history teacher. Sometimes Kelly had to admit to herself that Mrs. Hanson was a lot more than a teacher to her; Sandy Hanson was a friend, a buddy.

Not just a buddy, *sheesh*, Kelly had lots of buddies, lots of friends: Janice, Tara, the MoKid—especially the MoKid—but Mrs. Hanson wasn't just a friend, she was an adult. Ma didn't like Mrs. Hanson at all; she seemed to grate under Ma's skin, as if Ma was jealous of the time Kelly spent with her, but Kelly had a respect for her teacher which she didn't have for many people. She was responsible, she didn't just say or do things. She made decisions, she was a thinker.

Yeah, she was a *thinker*. Kelly wanted to be a thinker, too. Kelly wanted to be a teacher.

Melissa the MoKid questioned the logic of that.

15

"You really want to be knee deep in rug monsters?"

"Sure, why not? Kids are nicer than most adults."

"Not the ones I know." The thought of anyone actually wanting to hang around with small children amazed the MoKid, since she spent so much time trying to avoid baby-sitting for her younger brother and baby sister. "Being firstborn should not be the same as having the children yourself," MoKid frequently said.

"We all gotta do something," said Kelly, whenever they got into the discussion. "What's wrong with teaching?"

"Nothing, if you want to be like Hanson or McMurray."

"Which I do," said Kelly.

"Not me," said the MoKid. "I'd rather be like your mom. Carry a gun and beat heads."

"My mother does not beat heads."

"She could. She's a licensed headbeater."

That was something which always made Kelly wonder, how people could be born into the wrong families. Melissa the MoKid obviously would have been happy to have been born to Kelly's mother—*but what about with Doug the thug thrown in for the deal?*—and Kelly thought MoKid's parents were about as stable as anyone could dream for. Still, Kelly tried to keep everything in some sort of perspective. "Ma's a police detective. You read too much *Impossible Detective* magazine."

"I get them from your mother, trying to catch a

16

few crooks on my own time. Maybe you don't read enough.''

Who could stand it? Kelly wondered. She said, "*And* you watch too many movies.''

"So? You watch too much 'Muppet Babies.' Kids are not cute; they're messy, loud, and they get all the attention.''

"Sounds like the complaint of someone with a lot of younger brothers and sisters.''

"Sometimes I lose count.''

They both laughed; Kelly and Melissa the MoKid laughed a lot. Just like Melissa and Mrs. Hanson talked about things, except with the MoKid Kelly held back some things, embarrassing things. They were friends, but friendship only went so far. Ma was just her mother. With Mrs. Hanson, she could talk about anything. . . .

Which was so true that the same afternoon Kelly stopped by Mrs. Hanson's house and told her, "You should be a psychiatrist. Or Dear Abby, anyway.''

"I'm working on it.''

"Really? Which, being a psychiatrist or the Dear Abby thing?''

"I'm already Dear Abby to half the ninth grade since they signed me up as class advisor. *Here.*'' Mrs. Hanson was rooting through a laundry basket and handed over some towels to fold. She didn't live very far away, so Kelly stopped by to talk sometimes, and very often got drafted into the housework. It was okay, though, because Mrs. Hanson was the smartest person Kelly knew, and

17

she had so many interests: politics, art, movies, music—all kinds of music.

No wonder the students wanted her as class advisor, but Kelly wondered. "Is that mandatory? Do you have to do that?"

"Yeah, some of it. Not all of it." Mrs. Hanson explained. The year before, Mrs. Hanson not only taught American history, she worked on the Video Club, yearbook committee, and helped with the fall play and spring musical; this year before she got drafted as freshman class advisor she was begging off, allowing time only for her classes and a few dance committees. "I like the dances." She hung some permanent press on wire hangers. "I like watching the freshmen edge their way into the auditorium for the first time, boys on one wall, girls on the other."

Stacking towels, Kelly blushed. She remembered that wall. Curious, she asked, "So why are you so busy this year?"

Mrs. Hanson shrugged. "Like I said, I'm working on it. I just finished my master's degree."

"Yeah? That's great."

"Yeah, it is. And now I'm putting together application packets, and I'll have to do interviews."

"Interviews? For what?"

"Because I want to get my Ph.D."

"Ph.D.?"

"A doctorate."

"You're going to be a *doctor*? A psychiatrist?"

"No. A psychologist, maybe. Probably I'll just write, or teach. Then I might be able to go out to P.N.C. and teach night school."

"What?"

Mrs. Hanson was teasing. "Well, maybe my ambitions are a bit higher than that, but you've got to start somewhere."

"Doctor Hanson. That's wild."

"So there isn't as much time for the other nonsense, but I've always got time for dances. How come we don't see you and Bob at the dances anymore?"

Bob was Kelly's boyfriend. Maybe boyfriend was an exaggeration; they were dating, nothing serious. Shrugging, Kelly said, "Bob prefers to hang out."

"Hang out?"

"With his friends. Our friends. Well, usually *his* friends."

"So don't these friends like to dance?"

"I don't know. They like loud music, but they'd rather talk over it than dance."

"Too bad," said Mrs. Hanson. "Young people should dance."

"Do you dance?"

"All the time. Remember, Ginger Rogers did everything Fred Astaire ever did, only she did it backward while wearing high heels."

"Ginger *who*?"

"Astaire and Rogers. The dance team? Forget it." Mrs. Hanson poked a finger at her forehead, as if trying to remind herself. "If it hasn't been on MTV, they haven't seen it." She started lifting things to carry upstairs and Kelly got ready to leave. Mrs. Hanson took a second to ask a question, though, *the* question. "How's your mother?"

19

Hesitating just a bit, Kelly said, "She's fine."

"Is she?"

"No, of course she's not. She's crazy."

"Crazy." Mrs. Hanson weighed the word.

"She must be, right? Putting up with him?"

"Still that bad?"

"Sometimes. Sometimes not."

Mrs. Hanson nodded, contemplating all that.

"It's funny," Kelly said to her teacher. "She likes him and hates you. Explain that."

"I wish I could." Taking a deep breath, Mrs. Hanson said, "You know my offer still stands. We could call some people. You could even stay here for a while. You could—"

"Ma would go crazy."

"You said she was already crazy."

"I need to go," Kelly said, moving.

There was a pause. "Come by some Saturday and I'll show you a Rogers-Astaire tape," Mrs. Hanson finally said. "Show you what hoofing really is."

"Hoofing?"

"Hoofing. *Dancing*." Mrs. Hanson groaned. "Go home, Kelly, go home. You're breaking my heart."

"Sorry," said Kelly, laughing again. And she did go home, where Ma had just arrived herself; she worked dayshift, which was 7:00 A.M. to 3:00 P.M., investigating break-ins, burglaries, the occasional robbery and very occasional shooting, usually nothing very serious. There hadn't been a murder in Long Beach for almost nine months, knock on wood; that was the ironic part, Kelly always thought. Ma was a police detective and the most dangerous thing she faced every day was going home.

Today was a perfect example. Doug the thug was home, in a lousy mood. It always took him a few days to get over one of his blowups, and Kelly figured she knew why: guilt. He felt guilty about being a jerk, and the only way he was able to justify it was to convince himself the reason he was angry was he was being mistreated. So after he hit he growled for a couple of days.

Except this evening was different; Doug the thug didn't growl, he hit Ma again. And there was another first: when Kelly spoke up, stepped over to break up the nonsense, Doug the thug did something he had never, ever done before.

He hit Kelly.

From *Revenge Is Fun! A Guide to Destroying Your Enemies*, Zeus Publishing, New York, New York:

> The first step in crippling your enemies is knowing them, understanding their habits. Figure out what makes them enjoy life, then take it away from them. . . .

As found advertised in *Impossible Detective* magazine.

Double J—Jasper Jacobs High School—was located just off the downtown area of Long Beach, too far to walk, and since Kelly didn't drive, she rode the bus.

The bus was a nightmare. Most likely it was supposed to be, the mess and noise a calculated attempt to convince as many kids as possible to walk, thus making it cheaper to run the bus system. Save money and line somebody's pockets with cash, no doubt.

Kelly rode, as always, alongside Melissa the MoKid. "He hit me."

"What? *Oh my God.*" Horrified, MoKid looked her over quickly, instantly relieved, saying, "There's no marks."

"It was just a slap. I hate him."

Kelly was simmering, and the MoKid was impressed. "There's an accomplishment. Finally Knock-Knock Kelly actually hates somebody. I was beginning to worry about you."

Kelly almost smiled; it was a subject she and MoKid long debated, the *look for the bright side* perspective versus *the world is out to get you.* Or, as MoKid put it, *love thy neighbor but know thy enemy*. MoKid knew hers well enough, she even kept a list. "Got the idea from reading about Richard Nixon," she explained at the time. "When he was president he kept an enemies list, and I thought that was cool. And useful. So I thought up my own." Which she wrote down, amended, and constantly revised; there were currently thirty-nine names. She kept the list on the inside back cover of her notebook.

Kelly wasn't quite ready to start an enemies list, but she was upset. Mostly because she always bragged about knowing how people thought; Doug the thug was the exception, and Ma was working up to be one. "Why does he do this? He used to be the nicest guy in the world." Kelly told MoKid the story, the short version, but the retelling made her just as angry as anything else.

MoKid shook her head. "Forget about him, why he does it, your mother's the cop—the real question is why does she—"

"Who knows why she does; I don't."

"My dad never even spanked me."

"He's not my dad," said Kelly, correcting her. "My dad would kill Doug if he knew about this. Hey, there's an idea."

"Telling your dad?"

"No. Maybe I'll kill Doug the thug myself."

"Right."

"I could do it. Ma's got two guns, the one she takes to work and the one in the drawer at home."

MoKid grimaced; the bus pulled onto Elston Street; they were almost to Double J. "Don't say that too loud. If he turns up dead, it'll be your fault."

Kelly smiled. "I'd relish the defense."

Kelly was disappointed; Mrs. Hanson was out of American history. It was Kelly's second class of the day and she had been looking forward to talking to Mrs. H, venting a little more about Doug the thug. Kelly was class assistant; her third hour was a study hall and she frequently got to hang late— Mrs. H's third hour was prep time—and a lot of time she got to goof around, a hall pass greasing her into fourth hour.

Not this day. In Hanson's place a striking-looking young blond woman in black was leaning back against the file cabinet, and the name written across the blackboard read *Ms. Gwen Anders*.

She spoke when the class was only three-quarters full; students were still filtering in from the hall. Straight gold hair edged her high cheekbones and fell—in dramatic contrast—across the shoulders of her black sweater. "Everybody please take a seat and form an opinion."

"What?" Even Kelly found herself looking up.

"Settle down. Form an opinion. Make up your mind about something, and when the bell rings we'll take it a step farther."

Sheila Garland sat closest to the substitute, and she asked, "Make up our minds about what?"

"Anything. Something. Don't you have opinions?"

"Lots. We just don't know what you want."

"So what do *you* want?"

"Huh?"

The substitute settled behind Mrs. Hanson's desk, leaving the question open. Kelly figured since she was Mrs. Hanson's class assistant maybe she should help take charge, so she said, "You mean what do we want out of history?"

"History, life, whatever. Surely you want something."

Creeps answered now, and Kelly felt herself rolling her eyes at his answer before she even heard it. Creeps was a tense, nerdy boy known throughout the school for his obsession with horror movies and heavy metal music. He said, "I want to get out of laps in gym class."

"Why?"

"Because I hate them."

"Hate's a pretty strong word for something you simply dislike. Why wouldn't you want to run?"

"Because he's a wimp," said Terry Gallon.

This brought laughter, and Creeps defended himself. "No. It's boring."

The substitute considered this. "So, in your opinion, running is a boring form of exercise, although it does accomplish a purpose, in that it helps get you in shape for football."

"I don't play football."

"You should—I think you'd make a marvellous football player. You've the physique for it."

Creeps blushed.

Oh my God, thought Kelly. Creeps actually blushed.

The substitute was still caught up in her own analysis. "So. What would work just as well to achieve our aims, but be less boring?''

"I don't know. . . . "

"You should know what you're talking about. Uneducated opinions are just babble.''

"Sorry.''

"Temper your apologies. They come across as excuses, and I excuse no one.''

Wow, thought Kelly. This lady is really aggressive. Too bad she wasn't the one facing Doug the thug every evening—she'd clean his clock.

Addressing the class, the substitute said, "My name—as scrawled behind me—is Gwen Anders, and, as you've seen, I'm the substitute. I shall be here for two weeks—or so I'm told. Mrs. Hanson is going to be out on personal time.''

"Personal time?'' snorted Russ Hayes. "What does that mean?''

"It means it's none of your business.''

Creeps laughed; the jocks were having the worst of it for once, and that was fine with him, Kelly knew. Creeps usually got the worst of it. Never before had he seemed to show the slightest interest in school, but he was definitely smiling at the lovely Ms. Gwen Anders.

As were all the guys in class.

Serves them right, Kelly thought, not jealous but a little pleased. Let them lust after something they couldn't have, a beautiful woman in her late twenties, early thirties. Might teach some of them some humility.

Except Bob, her boyfriend, was among the drooling idiots. *Sheesh*, what a jerk. A cute jerk, but come on, Bob, grow up. . . .

27

Ms. Anders was pressing on, reviewing paper-work on her desk. "I understand I have a student aide for every hour . . ." She consulted a list in her lesson plan book, and looked up. "Kelly Wallis?"

"Me." Kelly raised her hand.

"Excellent. I need a little bit of help getting sit-uated, are you in any position to possibly help me after class for a few moments?"

"The whole hour if you need. All I have is study hall."

"Appreciated."

Somebody a few rows back made a wise remark, catching the substitute's glance. Kelly caught that it was Tyrone Tanner. "Please cease and desist with that nonsense. If you've something to say, at least have the courage to say it loudly enough to face rebuttal."

"Rebuttal?"

"Yes, or as I say, heckle the heckler."

The class laughed.

"Why do you talk so funny?"

"I'm sorry?"

"Why do you talk so funny? You sound goofy."

Shrugging, the substitute said, "Well, as I'm not quite sure our definitions of *goofy* would be com-patible, I'll take your question at its lowest possible meaning—you're insulting me."

"Huh? I—"

"Which is fine, perfectly, absolutely fine with me," said Ms. Anders, rising to her feet, stepping slowly around the desk, and reducing Tyrone to putty. "However, if you're open to honest sugges-tion, you might consider a more creative banter

28

than just tossing out words like *goofy*, or stupid, or dumb, ugly, stinky, lousy, whatever and whenever you're confused or can't think of anything to say. Try using your brain as an efficient tool rather than simply insulation to keep your skull from freezing in cold weather and you might achieve something more spontaneous—it's called *wit*."

Kelly was in awe. *This lady is so cool*. Realizing she wasn't even missing Mrs. Hanson, Kelly felt a little guilty, but the substitute wasn't quite finished. She was above Tanner's desk. "Tyrone, is it?"

"Yeah."

"We should speak further, you and I."

"Ho-ho-ho," chuckled Creeps. "Detention again."

"Going to offer me a detention slip?" asked Tyrone, smiling slyly up at Ms. Anders. "I think I could handle that. The punishment would not be so bad. . . ."

"No, I'm sorry," said the substitute, smiling an inviting, but oddly detached smile. "I never detain anyone. I prefer to simply and completely ruin their lives in ugly, ugly ways."

The class laughed again; Kelly too.

"So, shall we progress? Excellent." Returning to her desk, full attention back on the matter at hand, Ms. Anders lifted a textbook from the desktop and flipped idly through the pages. "American history, the history of America, two or three centuries of something or other. Where shall we ever pick it up at . . . ?"

From *Impossible Detective* magazine, July issue, page 167, classified section, Investigative Column:

MIAMI, FL: MANSLAUGHTER SUSPECT—bail jumper, $$$$ for info or capture, Jennifer Anne Fritch, age 27, 5' 11", wt 125, black hair, blue eyes, attractive with disfigured left hand. Contact Detect #331-21-3651.

Hanging back after class to help out, Kelly dug through Mrs. Hanson's debris and was surprised to find how disorganized it appeared when an outsider stepped in. With Mrs. Hanson around there seemed to be a system for everything; with Ms. Anders trying to fill in, she and Kelly were just two explorers in search of a lost lesson plan. Gwen Anders was grateful for the assistance. "You're really a lot of help. Appreciated."

"No problem. I like the way you handled Tyrone; that was so cool."

"Simply my way. How do you handle Tyrone?"

"I don't." That seemed an odd question. "I never need to handle him."

"He's never asked you out?"

"No."

Ms. Anders seemed surprised. "He appears the type who would."

Did he? Sure, Tyrone went out with a lot of girls, but Kelly had never actually wondered what it would be like to go out with him. *Had she?* "I'm sort of going with someone."

"Bob?"

That was a shocker. "Yeah—how did you know?"

Ms. Anders considered this a moment. "Well, either I'm psychic—which I'm not, no one is—or terribly perceptive on certain matters, which I am. I saw the way you looked at him every time he laughed at my jokes. He did laugh a little too hard."

"All the guys did."

"Ah—a little sincere jealousy."

"No, I was glad for it. I like to see these guys frustrated."

Ms. Anders nodded. "Well, Kelly—it was Kelly, wasn't it?"

"Yeah. That or Knock-Knock."

"Knock-Knock?"

Kelly explained. "When I was five I got real into knock-knock jokes, every one ever thought up, I think. I still know most of them."

"Really? Knock-knock."

Embarrassed, Kelly said, "Who's there?"

"Who huh."

What? "Who huh who?"

"Congratulations, you now sound like an owl with asthma."

"Funny."

"Anyway, I'm Gwen, and you needn't concern yourself with me. I promise not to steal your boyfriend." The substitute smiled again, holding out her hand; Kelly shook it. There were thick white scars on the underside of Ms. Anders's right wrist; both wrists actually. *Strange.* "What happened?" asked Kelly.

"Excuse me?"

"To your wrists. You . . ."

"Oh, my beauty marks." Ms. Anders held them both up; thick white lines, long since healed but striking in their contrast to the tanned skin around them; they gave Kelly the willies. "What happened?"

"This . . . well, this was a long time ago. My little accident."

Relieved—*why?*—Kelly said, "Accident?"

"Yes, I accidentally cut them."

"How?"

"Like this." Ms. Anders made a sudden, quick, violent slashing motion, first across the left and then the right wrist; it startled Kelly. "And then," said Ms. Anders, "and then I sat back in a warm bath and kicked on more hot water with my toes. Kept my hands under the water and bled and bled. . . ."

"Oh my God."

"Oh, yes. Have you ever perhaps wondered what it's like to cut your wrists? It's thrilling, like diving into an ice-filled bucket of water. And your body starts to get colder, too, because the blood takes the heat of the body away with it, but that's okay, too, because the hot water keeps you warm like a snug, cozy blanket on a frigid winter's night."

Shocked, Kelly stammered for the words. "But I thought . . . I mean, what . . . why would you try and kill yourself?"

"Quiet revenge."

"Revenge?"

"Yes." The substitute seemed to grow distant for a moment, and she said, "I wished to hide from someone, someone who hurt me more than I thought anyone could possibly be hurt, and I thought the only way to hide was to . . . well, I thought it was the only way to hide myself."

"From a man?"

"A monster. He was no man."

Kelly nodded. A *monster*. She knew her own share of monsters.

"It's quite therapeutic, really. There's something very cleansing about attempted suicide. Works all the bad stuff out of your system. I'll never try that again, that's for sure."

"That's good."

"Oh, yes." Ms. Anders nodded in all seriousness. "Take this lesson to heart, my message to you, young Kelly. There's no reason to turn on yourself with so many uglier targets in the world."

"I don't understand."

"Be your own best friend."

That was pretty much the same advice Mrs. Hanson always gave, and Kelly nodded. "I try. It's just . . . since Ma wound up with this new guy, Doug the—"

"Hmmm?"

She'd almost said *thug*, but instead Kelly said, "Doug the fireman. Ma worries after him more than she ever did my dad. She puts up with more. She's got less time for me than she ever had."

"Your mother remarried?"

34

"Yeah."

Ms. Anders seemed to understand that. "I had a husband once. They are an awful distraction."

"You're divorced?"

"Yes. He left me after . . ."

The substitute's voice trailed off, but Kelly asked, "After what?"

"After I was bound to be left. I never once blamed the man. Wished him nothing but joy."

"Joy."

"Yes."

"So where did you teach before?"

"Illinois, California." Ms. Anders chuckled, though it seemed almost forced. "I can't seem to hold a job these days. That's a joke."

Kelly nodded.

"Where did you go to college?"

"You've never heard of it. An all too obscure place called Antonmywer."

"In Oregon?"

"Yes. You've heard of it?"

Kelly was laughing. "Yeah, this is so weird. My mother went to Antonmywer, and my grandfather."

The substitute was shocked. "You're kidding."

"No, I'm serious. Wow. I always used to tease her that nobody outside the family ever went there."

Ms. Anders took this quietly enough; she didn't make much of a comment, anyway. Just nodded. "That's interesting."

"Yeah, wait'll I tell Ma." That was such cool news. For some reason she didn't understand,

Kelly felt herself opening up to Ms. Anders; maybe because the substitute had been so honest, so open with her. The suicide story was more a confession than anything else, unless it was a moral value lesson that she told everyone, the way alcoholics preached their drinking days to anyone who would listen. Maybe by talking about suicide all the time you helped ward away evil spirits.

Whatever the case, Kelly heard herself saying things about Ma and Doug the thug that she only told Mrs. Hanson, or Melissa the MoKid. "He hits her," Kelly said, dropping it very suddenly. "She's a cop and she still lets him hit on her."

Obviously surprised, Ms. Anders said, Your mother is a policewoman?"

"A detective, yeah."

"So why would such a strong woman allow herself to be subjugated by anyone?"

"That's what I want to know."

"Perhaps she's not as strong as she appears. My own inclination is toward insanity. I think it's right and proper to go a little crazy from time to time."

"You do?" Kelly didn't understand.

"Surely," said Ms. Anders. "Here's a historical note for you from your substitute history teacher. The American millionaire J. Paul Getty claimed to have three rules to live by, and he was constantly writing them down—on papers, charts, walls, napkins. The rules were: one—*get up early*; two—*work hard*; three—*find oil*."

"Oh, yeah?"

36

"Yes. My own rules are exactly the same save the last—instead of find oil I try to go a little crazy every day."

"Really?"

"Yes," said Ms. Gwen Anders, rubbing gently at the scars on her wrists. "Consider for a moment how much more interesting this world would be if we all lost our minds. . . ."

From *Revenge Is Fun! A Guide to Destroying Your Enemies*, Zeus Publishing, New York, New York:

Once you've decided to torment another human being, the hard psychological choices are over—now the fun begins! Whether you're simply submitting a fake change of address to reroute all of your victim's mail, spreading (and documenting) malicious and defamatory rumors, or taking the torture to the *supreme* levels (see chapter #6, *Booby Traps, Brake Lines, and Other Car Jokes*) the opportunities for amusement while reducing your opposition to pitiful cries for mercy are endless. . . .

As found advertised in *Impossible Detective* magazine.

It was with the advice of the substitute ringing in her ears that the next afternoon, after school, Kelly chose to lose her mind.

Which wasn't the only strange thing to happen that day; a strange thing happened in Mrs. Hanson's class, with the sub. Word of Ms. Gwen Anders had spread around Double J—as word of any interesting substitute would—and she was at the blackboard illustrating a point on the American Civil War when Jerry Slatter stepped in and snapped her picture.

"*Hold!*" Ms. Anders pointed and shouted before Jerry could take a step backward.

He was more than a little startled, saying, "What? What is it?"

"Who told you to take my photograph?"

"What? Nobody, I'm working to be a photographer. I . . ."

"Absolutely *not*. Surrender that camera. *Now.*" There was ice in Ms. Anders's voice; everybody in class noticed it, especially Kelly, and Jerry handed over the camera without even thinking.

"Absolutely not . . ." said Ms. Anders again,

39

opening the back and—before Jerry could object—cracking open the film container and ruining the raw film in the light of the room. She pulled and tore and balled the film up before tossing it into the trash and returning the camera. A lot calmer now, she said, "I'll pay for the film, of course. I'm sorry. Many cultures—mostly primitive, usually in Africa, South America, or Australia—believe that to take a photograph is to steal a bit of a person's soul. Well, I'm sorry, but I believe that as well."

"Gee . . . I didn't mean to . . ."

"Don't apologize. Find out how much to replace the film and I'll pay it at once."

"Sheesh, I'm sorry. Don't worry about it."

Jerry left then, and Ms. Anders carried on as if nothing had happened, but Kelly asked her about it after class as she helped her with a few things. Hearing the question, Ms. Anders hesitated a moment, but said, smiling as always, "Want a suggestion to help you through life's toils?"

"Yeah, always."

"Don't ask presumptuous questions on subjects which don't concern you."

Ice. Ms. Anders was ice, nice to ice, and Kelly went on to study hall, embarrassed and kicking herself. But the weirdness of the day was only beginning, because when she went home things went bing, bang, click, *whirr*, and Kelly decided to go ahead, take the sub's advice, and go insane.

Never before had Kelly considered that insanity could be a totally calculated decision, but when she arrived home again to the sounds of Ma in the kitchen—her mother, the tough police detective—

cowering to Doug the thug, something inside of her snapped.

Not so much snapped, perhaps, as sizzled.

Kelly's brain sizzled, and she decided, calmly, rationally, *okay, how about murder?* Commit a little murder and look for the bright side afterward.

So she went to her mother's bedroom and got the house gun.

Kelly wasn't afraid of guns, never had been, even with Doug the thug around. Ma was the cop and Doug was tough enough to slap around a woman who wouldn't hit back, but he was never going to move an inch toward one of the guns.

Kelly would, though; she decided that a long time ago, many long times ago, and she was doing it before she even realized her intention. The 9mm Beretta in the desk drawer; Kelly'd fired it several times before, Ma showed her how. The gun was unloaded, but the clip of bullets shared the same drawer and she knew how to get it inside; two easy movements. *Bang. Click.* Back with the bolt, and Kelly was in the kitchen almost before even leaving the bedroom.

"Don't you figure you . . ." Doug stopped talking. He saw Kelly now, Kelly and the gun, and this gave him just a second's pause. "Well now, Knock-Knock. Who do you think you are, Wyatt Earp?"

"Kelly . . ." Ma's voice was very calm, more than calm; she must have seen past the bravado and right into Kelly's heart, seen her seriousness. "Kelly, *don't.*"

"Maybe I should."

41

"Don't *what*?" Doug didn't sound as cocky now. He was questioning, and with the question he had to be nervous. "Is that thing loaded?"

Back with the bolt again, the first bullet ejected, flying across the kitchen, clinking on the tile; the next round slid into the chamber, ready to be fired. Kelly's hand squeezed on the trigger. . . .

"Hey, hey! *Easy!*" Doug's back thumped against the wall, but he didn't have anywhere to go.

"Kelly, don't. Please."

Ma was still reasonable, calm. Then Kelly wondered: was that the voice she used in police situations? Was that the voice she used on the kid she backed down at the 7-Eleven? Was that the voice she used, even as she was wishing she had just gone ahead and shot the guy? Kelly trembled, saying, "Call the captain."

"Kelly . . ."

"Call Captain Morris, call the station, call your police friends, call *somebody*. Lock this guy up."

"Kelly, he's leaving. Tonight. I swear."

Kelly trembled, again, but inside she felt very cold, very calm. Ms. Anders, the substitute, there was a strong woman, ready to go crazy for the fun of it, ready to go cold when annoyed; she was *tough*. What about now? Was this how Ms. Anders would handle a situation like this? For some weird reason Kelly was totally positive Ms. Anders would pull the trigger.

So, thought Kelly. Maybe she should just go ahead and shoot Doug; after all, even if Ma made him leave, he was going to wind up hitting some other woman. That was how guys like him got off, slapping smaller people around. Him the hotshot fireman risking his life for others, and guess where he found his real thrills.

But . . . *no*. Can't do it. Of course she couldn't do it.

Snap, *click*. Kelly pulled the clip from the gun, tossed it into the living room.

Doug the thug was on her in a second, right there with a vicious slap, and Kelly hit the wall but didn't raise a hand to protect herself; she didn't have to. Ma jumped in and took the pistol from her hand and pressed the barrel against Doug's forehead before Doug the thug could hit her again; she wasn't a wife now, she was all cop. "Hey, jerk."

"What? Hey!"

Ma pushed him back against the wall again. "You don't know anything about guns do you? There's still a bullet in here, a round in the chamber. Stupid, stupid, *stupid*. She could have accidentally blown a hole through you when you slapped her, without even meaning to. Like maybe I should now."

Doug the thug just shook his head, backing away. "You two are a pair. You're *both* crazy."

"Crazy."

"Crazy *sick*. I'm out of here."

"So go then."

"I am, I'm gone."

"So go."

And he did. He took fifteen minutes to pack a couple of things and Doug the thug bolted off into the night.

So be it, thought Kelly. So be it.

On the ride to school the next morning, the MoKid was very scared by the sound of the whole story. "Oh my God, what's going on?"

"Nothing's going on," said Kelly. "He's gone, finally. Thank God."

"Good. Maybe you'll stop being a maniac."

"No, I've got worse problems."

"What? You mean with Bob?"

"I don't know . . ." *Bob?* Kelly had actually been thinking about Ms. Anders and tried to clear her thoughts; she'd spent the whole night thinking, it seemed. About Doug the thug, about Ms. Anders, Bob, even about Tyrone Tanner—which was *weird*—except she'd found herself considering all the things Ms. Anders had suggested about him.

So Kelly felt her mind more than a bit muddled. "Boyfriend stuff. Terrific, that's all I need right now."

"Enjoy it while you can," said the MoKid.

"Right. I know I'm supposed to be worried a lot about Bob, and whatever, but I don't even know if I've got time for this."

"For what?"

"Going together. What does that mean, anyway? Why does everything have to be a big complicated relationship? Doesn't anybody just go out on dates anymore?"

Melissa the MoKid smiled. "I wouldn't know— What's a date?"

"Funny. You know what I mean."

"That's a nice little dramatic speech, don't you

44

think? If you want to break up, break up. You could go out with lots of guys.''

''I don't want to go out with lots of guys. If I break up with Bob, he's just going to be all hurt and I don't want to hurt him, but . . . I don't know what I want.''

''You wanted the thug gone. He's gone. Move on to the next thing.''

Kelly nodded. Good idea. Move on to the next thing.

Except . . . the next thing was not particularly great, either.

''Oh, and another thing,'' Ms. Anders announced to the class as the history hour drew to a close. ''I've decided to replace my classroom aide.''

What?

''Thank you for all your help, Kelly. My new assistant is Kenny Newlan.''

Kelly was too stunned to even think. Kenny Newlan? *Who?* That name was familiar but . . . *hey. Creeps?*

Kelly started to say, ''But I . . .''

''Let's discuss this after class, shall we? Everyone has their homework assignments, such as they are, but most of all I'm hoping for some intelligent, interesting discussion tomorrow. Concentrate. Form some opinions. I'm counting on you all.''

The bell rang then, and Ms. Anders stood at the door, smiling and waving everyone out. Kelly didn't move, didn't even rise from her desk as the classroom emptied. When everyone was gone she asked, "Why was I replaced?"

As always, Gwen Anders considered this a long moment before answering. "Well now. I'm not so sure how to put this diplomatically, so I'm just going to say it. Ethical reasons."

"Ethical what?"

"Ethical reasons. Ethical lapses, let us say."

"What does that mean?"

Ms. Anders nodded. "Well, the admin office gave me an inventory of what I should have access to and I found some supplies missing."

"What?" That didn't make any sense.

"I'm not saying it was you. Most likely it would be your teacher, wouldn't it? I mean, a student couldn't walk away with things unmonitored. I just wasn't about to sign on as recipient for several items which were actually unaccounted for."

That *definitely* didn't make any sense. "Mrs. Hanson would never steal anything. She had to buy most of the stuff with her own money anyway."

"Well, I guess that's most likely true."

"What is that supposed to mean?"

Ms. Anders chose not to explain. Instead she said, "I think you'd better hurry on, Kelly. I'm sure you have things to accomplish in your study hall."

"But why am I replaced? I didn't do anything . . ."

Hurrying out ahead of her, Ms. Gwen Anders said, "I have things to see in the teachers' lounge. . . ."

And so Kelly was left alone.

Or left *out* alone, depending on how you looked at it. And this bothered her, bothered her so much she was slow actually moving, actually heading on to study hall. She was late, but this time with no pass, no excuse, and Garrison, the student aide in charge, was more than happy to pencil out a detention slip for Mr. Masters's endorsement.

Whatever. Kelly had been dumped by a substitute teacher—big deal—except there was a plan to that stuff, a plan for everything Kelly worked for. Help out the teachers, get good letters of recommendation, scholarship help, get into a good college. There was a plan.

Kelly felt like her whole educational lifestyle was falling apart at the hands of a substitute with very strange mood swings, which was a stupid way to feel. So be it, she'd survive; Mrs. Hanson would be back in a few days and she wasn't likely to want to work with Creeps and his *Texas Chainsaw Massacre, Friday the Thirteenth Part 200* sense of humor.

So she'd been embarrassed by the lady. Big deal. She'd stay low and shut up and this would be over in a few days. So be it. And that might have been the worst thing Kelly had to contemplate the day after she chose to go crazy, except, when she got home that afternoon, Doug the thug was back. . . .

OPERATION TORMENT PAPERS, #11

Murder? No, But . . .

EXP. PRIVATE DETECTIVE/PERSONAL SECURITY Specialist KNOWS that sometimes someone needs to intervene on YOUR BEHALF. Battered spouses, abused children, exploited individuals, a PROFESSIONAL is available. Detect #117-01-2282.

From *Impossible Detective* magazine, August issue.

6

The next morning Ma stayed home late, after Doug left for work, and she was all explanations to Kelly at the breakfast table, calm and logical on the surface, although Kelly knew it was all a bunch of crap. "Doug has problems," Ma was saying. "He's aware of them."

"I don't believe I'm hearing this. . . ."

"We're going to get counselling. As a family."

"As a *family*? Ma, we're not a *family*; it's you and me and then there's *him*. I should have shot him when I had the chance."

"Kelly!" Ma slapped her, fast, sudden. "Don't ever think . . . don't ever *talk* . . ."

The blow stung, more from surprise than anything else. Kelly nodded at her mother, very cold. "So now we all get to play Doug the thug's game."

"What you said was wrong."

"Do what you want, Ma. I'm not staying around for this."

"No? What do you plan to do? Run down to your teacher friend's house? I told you I didn't want you hanging around there so much."

"You told me the thug was gone forever, too."

"Don't call him that."

"Ma, he's crazy."

"He's not crazy."

"Forget it, forget it, forget it," said Kelly, raising her hands and heading out through the living room. Kelly didn't wait for the bus. She didn't have a license, true enough, but she knew how to drive and she snapped the wagon keys up off of the sideboard—leaving Ma Doug's car—and drove herself to school. *Let them stop me*, she thought, mad, furious. *I can't get a ticket, my mother's a cop....*

She was one of the first to park in the Double J student lot, and that was no problem, but the problem was what Kelly saw in the teachers' lot as she walked—still steaming angry—around toward the front of the building. She saw that Ms. Anders, the substitute, was the first teacher there but Ms. Anders was . . .

Oh my God.

Ms. Anders was sitting in her car, being weird. Dangerously *weird*.

Keeping herself out of sight now—Kelly hadn't been seen, or else she had been and was being ignored—Kelly stood behind one of the big trash Dumpsters and watched, fascinated, as Ms. Anders sat behind the wheel of her vehicle, an expensive-looking white two-seater sports car, flicked a lighter, flame rising, and stuck her index fingertip into the flame.

Jumped. Seemed to bite her lip from the pain.

Then did it *again*. Same flame. Same finger.

Oh my God. . . .

Kelly almost felt like throwing up from what she was seeing—the woman was *sick*. Looking around for someone else who might be witnessing this, Kelly couldn't find anyone, and she watched for another moment as Ms. Anders sat in her car, continuing to singe her fingertip. God, it must be blistering by now. Or worse, *black*; the skin peeling . . .

Wasn't anyone else seeing this?

The substitute burned herself again, this time holding the finger to the flame a long while, longer, longer than anyone could possibly stand and Kelly heard herself make a sound—a coughing yelp mostly—and this time Ms. Anders looked up, toward her.

And smiled.

Oh my God. . . .

"Hey, Knock-Knock!"

Kelly jumped, but it was only Tara creeping up from behind; Tara rode a moped to school and always locked it up alongside the motorcycles. She wore a sturdy backpack instead of carrying a purse, and brushed frizzy red hair from her eyes. "What'd you do? Miss your bus? Can't be that, you're early."

"Look at this," said Kelly, quickly. "Look." She pointed Tara toward Ms. Anders's car, but it was empty. The substitute was nowhere to be seen.

"What? The car? That's a spider car, isn't it?"

Kelly sighed. "I don't know."

Tara pulled her by the sleeve. "Come on; Janice was bringing Dunkin' donuts. . . ."

51

Later that morning, in American history class, the substitute Ms. Gwen Anders wore a bandage on one of her fingers. "Don't you guys hate paper cuts?" she asked the class.

The rest of the school day was lousy—horrors in and horrors out, Kelly thought, more than a bit numbed by what she had heard and seen that day— but the MoKid was excited to hear that Kelly had the car. "Let me drive home," she begged as they cleared through their lockers and headed out.

"No way," said Kelly. On top of everything else her knee was bothering her and she felt a little cranky.

"Why not?"

"Because you don't have a license."

"So? You don't either."

"Yeah, but my ma's a cop. I'm invincible."

"Hardly invincible. She'll probably kill you for taking the car."

"She can't kill me."

"So she'll ground you for life."

"She can't ground me, either."

"Yeah? So why can't she?"

"It's a bright side thing," said Kelly, voicing her thoughts as they made more and more sense to her when spoken out loud, knowing she must have sounded like a wise guy. "When you're forced by your ma to live in the same house with a maniac, the bright side is the rules no longer apply. . . ."

*   *   *

Which may or may not have been true. After she got home Ma first exploded about Kelly taking the car, calmed, then tried again to convince her that everything was going to get better, that she had problems too, that she needed some help and concern. "Look, Kelly, I've got a case going right now."

"A real one, or just one of those leads out of *Impossible Detective*?"

Ma frowned. "I don't need these distractions, you know. I'm under a certain amount of pressure of my own."

"Pressure doesn't explain it all, Ma."

"No," said her mother after a long moment. "No, it doesn't."

Doug the thug came through the door then, tossing his gear onto the couch as he passed through, stopping in the kitchen for a beer and reappearing in the doorway. That was an awkward moment, as he stood there and—for Ma's benefit, Kelly was sure—attempted to speak with her. "Listen, Knock-Knock, I know I . . ."

Kelly wasn't up for this. "Could you not call me that?"

"What?"

"Could you not call me Knock-Knock anymore? It's childish and I don't want to be like that anymore."

"We're just trying to all get along," said Ma.

"I saw my substitute teacher at school today, and she was sitting in the parking lot burning her finger with a lighter." Kelly tossed this out mostly as a diversion; she didn't want to talk about the other stuff.

It was an effective diversion, though. Ma and Doug both stood up straight. "Excuse me?"

Kelly said it again, very slowly. "She was burning the tip of her finger with a cigarette lighter."

Doug the thug frowned. "You saw this? You're sure."

"I saw it. It was *so* sick."

Ma contemplated this as well.

"Why would a person do something like that?"

"I have no idea," said Ma.

"Do you think I should tell somebody?"

Doug snorted. "Like who?"

"I don't know. Somebody at school; Mrs. Hanson, maybe."

"Enough, enough about the great and glorious Mrs. Hanson," said Ma. "I remember the afternoon you told me this new substitute was the greatest thing since sliced bread."

"Yeah, but that was before all this. This can't be normal."

"That depends on who's defining normal."

"*I* am," said Kelly.

"You actually saw her intentionally burning herself?"

"Yes. She was sitting alone in her car with a lighter."

"And you were spying on her?"

"No, I just saw. I'm not blind."

Doug said, "You must have seen wrong. Maybe she was trying to dry her fingernails or something."

"With a cigarette lighter? For your information, Joe Fireman, fingernail polish is flammable."

"Maybe it was something else, I don't know. I can't imagine anyone burning themselves on purpose. I've seen people with bad burns. Nothing hurts worse."

"She told me she tried to kill herself once. She told me all about it."

This surprised Ma. "You're kidding."

"No. There's something very bizarre about this woman."

"I don't know," said Doug. "Sounds as if you're just wired up about this lady because she fired you as student aide."

Kelly felt as if she was catching the third degree from two sides at once. "It isn't."

"I don't know. I've noticed something about you, Knock-Knock. You either love your teachers so much that you go do their laundry for them, or else you hate them."

"I don't hate anybody."

"That's true, my mistake. You've got this big love thing. You need all your teachers to love you, you want everybody to love you, and one person doesn't. So what? What's the big deal? Is this lady not normal just because she doesn't love you?"

"I didn't do anything to her. I need to get out of here." Kelly got up.

"So is that your solution to everything these days? Run away?"

"Doug . . ." Ma tried to run interference. Kelly didn't need the help and wasn't sure if she even appreciated the effort anymore. "I'm already gone," she said.

So Kelly left home again, but this time she didn't get the car and, besides, she had no place to go.

First she walked down to the mall, which wasn't so far, about a mile and a half, and the weather was nice. Cool fall weather, leaf burning weather in the neighborhoods. The only problem was her knee was killing her by now, and she crossed the big parking lot at the highway intersection to sit in the mall a while and window-shop from the vantage point of the Food Court—a ring of fast-food places surrounding a battery of tables—but the only person she saw down there was Tyrone Tanner.

Which was interesting, sort of, the way he stopped talking to his friends and watched her as they walked by, but Kelly was alone—she tried calling the MoKid, no answer, and Janice and Tara were both out on dates. She almost called Bob, stopped herself because she suddenly felt tired, but that didn't mean she wanted Tyrone Tanner so obviously checking her out, did it?

Did it?

So she left the mall and went down to Mrs. Hanson's house, despite the face that she felt a little guilty about it, despite the fact that Ma was on her so much lately to stop hanging out over there. Kelly figured she'd just drop by to see if she was around, see what was going on. Except the house was dark, there was only one light on inside—deep inside the house—but the side door was open. The one that went in through the kitchen.

Kelly knocked on the open door. "Mrs. Hanson? Hello?"

No answer.

Just a suddenly creepy, eerie silence. Usually Mrs. Hanson had music; music on the stereo, or an old musical on the video. Now there was nothing: it was quiet.

Quiet as death.

Feeling a chill, Kelly pushed on the door. It swung inward easily, and she stepped through the doorway. She tried the kitchen light switch, and it came on but what she saw in its glow was the living room—the tall living room lampstand had been knocked over somehow, and when Kelly went to right it she found the plug-in cord for the lamp had been torn out at the base.

It was missing.

The clock radio lay on the floor flashing over and over 1:20, 1:20, 1:20. An hour had passed . . . since what?

What was going on?

Kelly ventured down the hallway, the same hallway she'd helped put linens and towels away in. The bathroom door was shut, and she knocked. "Mrs. Hanson? Hello?"

No answer, except there was a sound now, coming from farther down the hall. A squeak, a deep distinct *squeak*. What? It sounded like a door hinge. No, not a door hinge. Something else.

Squeak. Squeak.

"Mrs. Hanson?"

Still no answer.

Kelly opened the bathroom door, found it empty,

pulled it shut again. Wandered down the hall, toward the only other light, the one in the back bedroom.

"Mrs. Hanson? Hello? The door was open, and I . . ."

Kelly stopped talking.

Stopped breathing.

After a few minutes she stopped screaming.

Secured by the long lamp cord brought from the living room, Mrs. Hanson was hanging in the closet, her mouth open in a soundless gasp, her dangling feet barely six inches off the floor.

Her eyes were open.

From Cynthia C. Talbott's *Note Scrawled On The Morning After The Suicide Of A Good Friend*:

Wondering if my phone rang, if I wasn't around to answer your call, will always trouble me, but my soul won't shrivel; I'm not going to destroy myself, am I? With so many hopeless questions needing to be pressed, what's one more proposition worth the extra wonder. Except—

I never knew you were in such a hurry to move on. . . .

The world ended for Kelly Wallis all the time, no big deal, remember—the occasional doomsday was good for building character. When your father was gone, your mother a cop, her new husband a violent flake, and your friends didn't—could not—understand that you were dying on the inside . . . well, you needed to keep to the bright side. You had to move on. . . .

On the day Mrs. Hanson was to be laid to rest Kelly awoke crippled; her bad knee was hurting so badly she couldn't place weight on it, even with crutches, so she didn't get to go to the cemetery.

Some horror. Kelly spent the day alternating tears of frustration, humiliation, and grief. Finally, at around three o'clock, Ma appeared in the doorway to announce that someone was there to see her.

It was Gwen Anders, the substitute. Ma left them alone as the substitute stood, embarrassed it seemed, in the doorway. Her dress was black, so obviously she had been to the services, which surprised Kelly. *Why would she go? Why would she care?*

"I just came by to see if you were all right," Ms. Anders said, as if reading Kelly's thoughts.

"I hurt my knee a long time ago," said Kelly as coldly as she could make the words come out.

"Yes, that's what your mother said."

"I guess this means you've got a permanent job now, huh?"

"What?"

"With Mrs. Hanson gone it means you get to

keep the class for the rest of the year, doesn't it?''

"I don't know."

"Don't you?"

Ms. Anders stared Kelly boldly in the eye. "No, I don't."

"Whatever."

"I just came to see if you were all right."

"You said that already."

"So I did."

"You didn't even meet her."

"What?"

Kelly said it again. "You didn't even meet Mrs. Hanson, you didn't even know her. Why would you go to her funeral?"

"I felt responsible."

"*Responsible?* What do you mean responsible? You mean for her dying like that?"

"No," said Ms. Anders, "I felt responsible for her students. My students. *Our* students . . ."

"*Our* students?" Kelly felt angry, and for a split second wondered what she was so angry for. *Was she frightened for herself.* What she said was, "A teaching team with one in the grave, eh?"

"Kelly . . ."

"Kind of a bloody way to make a living."

"Bloody?"

"It's still Mrs. Hanson's class," said Kelly, the tears coming again, suddenly, surprising her. "You can take over if you want to, if you need to, but it's still going to be Mrs. Hanson's class."

The substitute actually nodded at that. "I know," she said.

61

The first, and *last Operation Torment Paper*:

"PROTECT THE ONES YOU LOVE!"

As torn from the inside cover page of *Impossible Detective* magazine.

The weeks following the funeral passed slowly; September became fall, and with the coming of October brown and yellow leaves cluttered the curbs and sidewalks. Kelly knew; she was doing a lot of walking. In the evenings the air smelled of dampness and burning leaves, although there were no obvious fires. Best of all was the wind. At first it was a simple breeze, shuffling through the trees, creating a whisper in its wake, but the more she watched, the tree branches seemed not to be bouncing gently in an invisible current, but rising and falling as waves; the simple trees not so simple anymore, but giant deciduous beasts, sulking in silence. Probably hatching plots against their world's tormentors, the stuff of nightmares.

And Kelly was having a lot of nightmares.

Knock-knock, knock-knock, who's there . . . ?
Kelly—Kelly, please.

Mrs. Hanson, wrapped in the film haze of a dream, wide-eyed as she was in her death, pleading with Kelly.

They found Mrs. Hanson hanging in her closet,

as Kelly had, dangling from a lamp cord, a typed suicide note at her feet. Which didn't make any sense to Kelly, except maybe it did. Mrs. Hanson was a creative person, and creative people took their own lives all the time, didn't they? Except Mrs. H had so much to live for, she was really excited the last time Kelly saw her—Mrs. Hanson was going for her doctorate, she was going to be Dr. Hanson.

Except she had been away from school for the previous week. How did Ms. Anders refer to the absence? "Personal time."

Ms. Anders, the substitute who was going to be subbing for the entire year now, it seemed. Ms. Anders, the real expert on suicide, Kelly knew; the woman with the nice white scars on her wrists and strange habits with a cigarette lighter.

Except it was Mrs. H who did it.

Or was it?

Chilling thoughts, but Kelly was ready for them when she woke up in the midst of a thunderstorm, rain pelting the rooftop and her knee hurting. Mrs. H left a note, but the reasons listed were bogus, Kelly knew; the note claimed that Mrs. Hanson, in a fit of depression over learning her ex-husband had remarried, decided life was too painful to bear.

Which was nonsense, Kelly knew that much herself. Not only was Mrs. H more than pleased to be rid of her husband, they had parted friends, wishing each other well, the same as Ms. Anders the substitute claimed. Kelly remembered passing this along to Ma, both of them amazed that one didn't have to hate a former lover. Not to mention the fact that he'd been married for three months—did it take three months for the onset of suicidal depression?

Mrs. Hanson wasn't depressed—the substitute, Ms. Anders—*she* was depressed. Mrs. Hanson was fine, happy, cheerful, right up to . . .

Right up to the day she killed herself.

"That's the way it is sometimes," Ma had assured Kelly. As a police officer she'd had some training in the matter, and people on the verge of suicide often went through emotional upswings— once past the decision to actually take their own lives, the actual execution was a formality. The burden gone, the depressed celebrated, right up until they did in themselves.

But Mrs. Hanson was like that all the time. Even in Kelly's dreams. *"I didn't, I didn't, you know I didn't. You know I wouldn't do this to you. . . ."*

Who would?

Third gear.

Fourth.

They were riding in the car, Kelly and Ma—it was Friday night the second week of October, a *we need to talk* ride since Kelly was making no effort to get out of the house, get out with her friends, get out of the *shell* she'd been in since Mrs. Hanson died—but her mother never took her foot off the gas, or her eyes off the road.

"Ma . . ."

"You've got to understand I have problems, too."

"I do understand," said Kelly, trying to sort out

her thoughts. They seemed unsortable.

Ma blew through an intersection; Kelly looked around. "You know you just ran a stop sign?"

"We survived, didn't we? We made it?"

"Yeah, we made it." Kelly let it go. Driving fast always made her mother feel better, and she wanted Ma to feel better, but now she wondered why it worked that way.

Did Ma need to risk herself? Risk both of them?

She was talking. "Listen, Kelly, I realize I and Doug have serious problems, but if you remember right you remember that your dad and I had problems, too."

"The same kind of problems?" There was a horrible possibility Kelly had never even imagined. "Did Dad hit you?"

"No," said Ma, after a moment's concentrated driving. "He never hit me. Not with his hands, anyway. He knew how to hurt much better than that."

"What do you mean?"

"What I mean is I need your help."

"Great," said Kelly, deciding to sort her thoughts by laying them all out in the open. "I need help, too."

"How?"

"It's about school. This substitute teacher we've got, Ms. Anders. The one who came over to the house. She's starting to really scare me."

"Scare you how?"

"Well—"

"*Damn.*"

Ma was cursing because, behind them, blue-and-white flashing lights had just snapped on, a patrol car.

"Oops," said Kelly.

Ma pulled over, switched the power window down. Behind them the uniformed cop crawled out of his car and walked up, aiming a flashlight in at them. "License and registration, please," he said.

Ma pulled her shield from her pocket and flashed it. "Detective Sergeant Wozniak," she said.

Wallis, Kelly thought, wishing and remembering for the old days. Detective Sergeant Wallis.

The patrolman relaxed, a fellow policeman. "Oh, hi, Sarge. Sorry about that, but the way you blew by . . ."

"No problem."

The uniformed cop was bored and talkative, and since he was obviously not going to write her a ticket Ma amused him a few minutes with chitchat while Kelly didn't get her chance to talk about what was really on her mind. The patrolman was up for the sergeant's test and wanted advice. "Is there a lot of constitutional law stuff on there?"

"More arrest procedures, bookings, process stuff."

"Hey, yeah."

They talked for a while longer before he waved her off and Ma drove them home, apparently comfortable with Kelly understanding her and Doug. Except Kelly considered her thoughts still unsorted, and didn't understand it. Not one little bit.

The next morning, Saturday, Kelly answered the side door and Melissa the MoKid walked immediately in, settled down at the kitchen table, her head falling into her hands. "Oh, God, what have you got to eat?"

"Eggs," said Kelly, returning to the book she'd been reading at the table.

"Eggs? You're going to cook me some eggs?"

"I never said I'd cook. Have at it."

"Fine." MoKid got up and dug through the lower cabinets, found a pan and started the motions of frying eggs. Midway through the process she goofed, loudly declared them scrambled, and demanded pepper and butter. "For effect."

"For effect?"

MoKid collapsed back at the table, the plate of eggs before her. "This is close to the effect I was looking for. Don't you eat in the mornings?"

"I eat when I'm hungry. I eat ice cream sometimes."

"Ice cream?"

"It's milk. It's good for you."

"Not for breakfast."

"So what about you? Eggs are just liquid chicken."

"And tasty."

"Gross."

Kelly closed up her book and watched MoKid eat for a while. She seemed to be really enjoying it. For Kelly, most food was flat and tasteless these days. MoKid talked a little about what Janice and Tara were up to—"I think we should go down to the mall, down to the arcade"—and she was about to say something else when Kelly killed the conversation once again by saying, "I don't think Mrs. Hanson killed herself."

"Kelly . . ."

"I refuse to believe that."

"I know you do. But you have to."

"Why?"

"Life goes on."

"Life doesn't go on, Mo. Mrs. H would never have killed herself, she never even said once anything about killing herself."

"How would you know?" asked the MoKid. "Who knows about suicide?"

"I know somebody," said Kelly, realizing *yes, yes, she did.* "I know somebody who knows a lot about suicide. . . ."

For a long time Kelly watched Ms. Anders, the way she walked, stood, talked when she was around the guys of the class. It was different than the way she was around the girls, but then again it wasn't different. Nothing she could peg a label on, nothing you could toss out any accusations about.

Except all of a sudden Creeps was acting almost like a human being—*almost*—and that was totally out of character. Creeps had some focus now, something to live for, but even that was weird, sick. Who lived to be the class assistant?

Me. There was an embarrassing truth to suddenly have pop into your head, but Kelly knew it was true. It was exactly the sort of thing she used to live for herself.

*   *   *

At lunch Monday Kelly sat with Bob and Melissa the MoKid; Bob thought she was being paranoid, and the MoKid wasn't voicing opinions. "I dislike all attractive single women from age eighteen to thirty-five, so I'm prejudiced."

"She's not single, she's divorced. There's a difference. And she's closer to forty."

"She acts like she's young and single, so it's the same thing." The MoKid ate a french fry.

"I think you're just mad because she took away your stupid job," said Bob.

Kelly stared hard at her alleged boyfriend. "Why does everyone keep saying that? I don't care about the job. Don't you think Creeps is turning into a strange person?"

"Creeps was always a strange person. What's the difference?"

"He acts like her slave. Like he wants to be her slave."

"I wouldn't mind being her slave myself."

"Bob . . ."

"Hey, Kelly, I love you, but I'm not blind and she's not invisible."

"So what is it with you guys? Your hormones make your brains inoperative? Can't you even think?"

"What is there to think about? Why are you acting so worried."

"I think . . ."

"What? You think what?"

"I don't know what I think."

"Take it easy."

Kelly looked out the cafeteria window instead.

Outside it was threatening to rain again, a drizzle if not exactly an Indiana monsoon, and the effect on Kelly's mood was easy to gauge; bad weather always made her leg hurt. "Just like somebody's grandfather," MoKid always teased.

Janice, Tara, and the twins Carl and Victor joined them at the lunch table; the twins played basketball and looked the part. Janice and Tara spent a lot of time looking up to them. MoKid immediately confiscated several french fries from Tara and Janice asked a question about band practice; Bob was also in the band, and thought he knew the answer. Everybody chirped about their business.

Kelly's business was starting to make her a little crazy.

Wonderful. Nothing like becoming the table geek, she thought, and for a while she managed to say nothing about Mrs. Hanson's death, or the substitute Gwen Anders. For a while Kelly played the part, and she said, as if chatting up idle gossip, "Did you guys hear about Mike Lisakk? He wracked up his motorcycle and broke his arm. . . ."

After school, Bob wanted to go get something to eat and the MoKid wanted to check out the mall for a while, but Kelly felt as if her brain was on overload; she said no to everybody and caught a ride with Tara down to Doolin' Park. Tara lived down that way anyway, and Kelly rode on the back of her moped; how she was going to get home she'd figure out later.

Doolin' Park bordered the lakefront—complete with two marinas, recreation fields, a few places to eat, and the Doolin' Park Zoo. The zoo was a point of interest, built in the 1930s as one of President Roosevelt's work programs to help ease the country out of the Depression, it had, over the years, been allowed to fall apart and become—according to an animal magazine in the 1970s—one of the ten most disgraceful zoos in the nation, an ugly place where the animals lived miserable existences in horrible cages.

No longer, thanks to Mrs. Fitzby.

Theresa Fitzby was—before her death in a motorcycle accident at age eighty-three—a Long Beach resident with more hobbies than time, and more available money than hobbies (her father was one of the original Indiana partners of Standard Oil). Her attention drawn to the Doolin' Park Zoo, Mrs. Fitzby updated her will, and when she spun out of a turn short one rainy Saturday afternoon the zoo found itself the beneficiary of nearly twenty-two million dollars—contingent on two things. One, all the money be spent on facilities and animals, and two, all the money be spent within eighteen months. Mrs. Fitzby was not remembered as a patient woman.

"So, thank you, Mrs. Fitzby," said the town newspaper on the day the newly remodeled zoo was reopened to the public. "The bears do." The bears being the Kodiak, black, and polar bears who were released from their tiny cement hell-cages to the habitats Mrs. Fitzby's money provided.

The tigers thanked her as well, Tony and Vessie, the bright and colorful pair of Bengal tigers allowed to roam free in a natural big cat habitat which could be viewed either from high above— the vantage a protected walkway the animals couldn't possibly leap to—or from slightly below the reinforced Plexiglas walls showing the critters living large.

Kelly liked the zoo.

She liked the zoo because it was never busy this time of year, and it was quiet but not too quiet, not so silent as to force one's thoughts to come crashing in on oneself.

Thoughts about Mrs. Hanson, Ma and Doug, the substitute.

Especially the substitute.

What was with her?

"Come on, come on," Kelly said out loud as she wandered the zoo, enjoying even the animal smells; *she wasn't becoming one of those obsessive people, was she?* She wasn't going to let Mrs. Hanson's death ruin her life, *was she?* No matter how important Mrs. H had been to her . . .

It was down by the lower level of the tiger sanctuary that Kelly bumped into Creeps. He was tracing his fingertips along the glass wall, trying to locate the cats, and he was growling. . . .

Creeps. Kenny Newlan, the frightmeister himself, standing there before the environment in his slasher movie T-shirt and cutoff denim jacket and jeans; Creeps also wore black cowboy boots with sharp-pointed toes. Now he shoved his hands in his pockets, still growling from deep in his throat.

BENGAL TIGER (*PANTHERA TIGRIS*) read the sign, but Kelly ignored all the description written below; she wanted to talk to Creeps. "Hey," she said.

"Hey." He seemed surprised to see her suddenly standing beside him, and Kelly used that to her advantage. "I didn't know you came to the zoo," she said. "I thought you preferred horror movies and stuff."

Creeps was quiet a long moment, then said, "I like lots of things."

"Me too."

"Yeah. I know about the stuff you like."

"You do?"

"Yeah." Staring hard at her now, Creeps's eyes had a defiance Kelly never remembered seeing in them; certainly not in the eyes of the Creeps who occasionally needed to borrow notebook paper, or a pencil. If anything, he might have somewhere shot down a jock with this kind of look; Creeps wasn't the sort to confidently take on a girl; his brain was in too much of a buzz.

Not now, or at least not so much; Creeps looked away from her, but not from shyness. It was a dismissal.

"Hey," she said again.

"What?"

"Nothing. I just . . ."

"You just what?"

Kelly tried to summon an idea, or at least a reasonably coherent thought. *No luck.* "I don't know. I was just surprised to see you down here. I like the zoo; I didn't know you did."

"So why would you care?"

"Sheesh, relax. What's the big deal?"

"There is no big deal," said Creeps. They both stared up at Tony as the giant cat made an appearance, restless and tense in his captivity, despite the many efforts to make it seem a pleasing, pleasant wilderness. *What sort of life was this?* Kelly often wondered, and Creeps went ahead and said so, saying, "Sometimes I want to figure out a way to get Tony and Vessie out of there."

"They'd probably eat you."

"Maybe. But then I'd be a part of them, wouldn't I?"

"What? I don't follow you."

"Think about that," said Creeps. "We are what we eat, and what we eat is part of us. If I eat a banana or some Twizzlers, they're part of me. If a tiger ate me, I'd get to be a part of a tiger."

"That doesn't make any sense."

"I'm not trying to make sense. Just dreaming. Don't you wonder what that would be like? Being a big beast, king of the jungle?"

"He's not king of the jungle. Just a tiger in a cage."

"All that energy ready to spring if he ever gets out."

"This is a town, not a jungle."

"Every town is a special kind of jungle."

"Maybe," said Kelly, a little bit nervous by the turn the conversation was taking. "So what's the deal with you and Ms. Anders?"

"Why?"

"Just asking."

"What do you care? You had your turn."

"Turn?"

"You were teacher's pet, now somebody else gets a turn and it bugs you, doesn't it?"

"No. I was just wondering." Except that wasn't really true; Kelly had a reason for wondering, and the way Creeps looked at her made her think he *knew* that she *knew*. Or maybe not *knew*, but suspected.

Suspected why the tips of three of Creeps's fingers had burn blisters on them. . . .

So Kelly gave it all a lot of thought, and the more she did, the more what happened to Mrs. Hanson—*Sandy Hanson! A human being, not just a teacher!*—seemed less like an accident—a *suicide*—and more like . . . well, like something else.

What? *Murder?*

Yes. Murder.

Unless she was forcing this, trying to make it murder in her head because she didn't want to accept the fact that maybe Mrs. H did kill herself, maybe she was depressed.

No way. Kelly knew she wasn't forcing this, wasn't building this into something, and one of the ways she knew were all the stacks of *Impossible Detective* magazine Ma had in the house. Kelly always hated them before—their pages sprawled with blood and killings and *America's Most Wanted*–type ads where every flake in the country could turn bounty hunter and rat out his neighbor for fun and prizes—

Except now it made more and more sense. There were an awful lot of sick people out there in the world. Her substitute teacher—Ms. Gwen Anders—was obviously one of them. Just the thing with the fire—the obvious time she tried to kill herself. *What did she do to Mrs. Hanson? How did she do it?* How could anything like this ever be found out, ever be proved?

Operation Torment. *Was it time?*

Operation Torment was something the MoKid had developed for Kelly long before, a thick loose-leaf notebook full of clippings and lists and plans—a lot like MoKid's enemies list, but more detailed; an actual battle plan culled from the pages of that horrible *Impossible Detective* magazine. Originally, *Operation Torment* was a scheme of retribution and revenge aimed at Doug the thug in retaliation for all his terrors; Kelly dismissed it as a good joke, but that was all until she started to get murder on her own brain. Revenge seemed better than murder.

But what if Gwen Anders was everything—or anything—Kelly feared she was. If she did this to Mrs. Hanson—

Where to start?

The answer she came up with—in between conflicts with Ma and the thug—was, obviously, Antonmywer. That was the college Ms. Anders went to, the same college as Ma, and if something was weird, as she knew most definitely it was, maybe it started way back there.

For answers, Kelly needed to go to the attic; a lot of Ma's stuff was still up there from the last move, the move from Chicago. Ma started her cop career in the Chicago Police Department, putting in her time as a college-educated patrol officer before she moved to plainclothes and, with the move to Long Beach, detective sergeant. Detective lieutenant was just months away now, Kelly knew, and she had no doubt that—barring any stupidity from Doug the thug—her mother would someday be running a police department. Maybe not the one in Long Beach, but somewhere, definitely, probably one of those horrible towns the stupid magazine was always visiting.

Still, the answers to the immediate questions lay in the attic, where several never-unpacked boxes remained from the Chicago homestead. Kelly was pulling down the overhead ladder to venture up there with a flashlight when Doug wandered through, asking what she was doing. He wasn't mean or rude, certainly not demanding; he was just asking the obvious question out of curiosity on seeing someone climbing a ladder with a flashlight, but just the gall of that infuriated Kelly; she had to grit her teeth to answer Doug the thug.

"What are you looking for?"

"Some stuff my dad gave me," she answered. That should set him back and off, and it did; Doug the thug made a hasty enough retreat and Kelly climbed toward the hot musky darkness of the attic space. There were lots of cartons stacked away up there; going through them all would be a real pain, but she knew the most likely place to find what she wanted was an old wooden chest, handed down from Grandma, and she was right.

The yearbook was at the bottom of the chest, and Kelly dug it out. THE ANTONMYWER CHASER, Kelly read with the flashlight. Ms. Anders had said she was two years behind Ma, and this was her mother's senior yearbook, so Kelly flipped through the black-and-white pages to the sophomore class. Assuming Anders wasn't a married name—*and she used Ms., right*?—Anders should be toward the front of the alphabet, right?

Right.

ANDERS, GWENDOLYN, said the listing to the left. Kelly scanned the pictures, not recognizing any but counting—it should have been third from the left. And there was a woman there, a Gwen Anders, but . . .

"No way." Kelly heard herself talking out loud, and said it again. "No way."

The Gwen Anders pictured was dumpy-looking, overweight, with a thick nose and horn-rimmed glasses. And black hair. Maybe a person could change a lot, but could she change this much?

Maybe. Come on, be fair, be logical; Kelly had to allow for what was possible, didn't she?

Dieting. That was easy, a woman could lose the weight. And the hair, that could be bleached out. And contact lenses eliminate the glasses, and a little slice of the plastic surgeon's knife takes care of the nose problem.

Make some allowances. Make a lot of allowances. Could the woman in the picture be Gwen Anders?

"No way." Kelly said it again, but this time she didn't repeat herself in the empty crawl space.

Still, this didn't prove anything, and maybe it shouldn't. Maybe the picture was wrong for a lot of logical reasons, maybe they made a printing mistake all those years ago; Kelly knew that was possible. Her junior high school yearbook inverted three different sets of pictures and left a few out altogether. Anything was possible.

Tucked into *The Antonmywer Chaser* was something interesting, though; a card from the *Antonmywer College Locator*, a service provided by the alumni organization. If you wanted to find somebody who attended the college, you called the locator service; Ma used it from time to time to locate a buddy. So Kelly crawled down from the attic and tried.

Clearing her throat a little, Kelly shifted the phone from right ear to left and explained who she was looking for, the information she had, and said, "I'd like to know how to get hold of her."

The woman from the alumni association hesitated. She'd just finished her file check and said, "I'm afraid that won't be possible."

"Why not?"

"I can't release that information."

"Why not? Does she say not to?"

"No, but . . . I'm sorry, but according to my records here, our only Gwen Anders died in 1991. . . ."

CHANGE YOUR IDENTITY

SPECIALTY AGENCY CAN ASSIST YOU IN BECOMING SOMEONE ELSE. Want to hide from the world? Disappear? Escape your past and start fresh? FREE INFORMATION PACKET! Detect #877-22-1182.

From *Impossible Detective* magazine, September issue.

10

Kelly had to tell somebody. MoKid wasn't home, and Tara and Janice were never home, so she wound up talking to Bob on the phone.

Which almost brought back pleasant memories; almost. Bob was all right—kind of cool, really—and she'd spent a few hours talking with him over the summer but now things were, well, *changing* between them. Just the idea of him didn't seem as exciting as it had before, when she used to find herself bouncing around the house waiting for him to call, thrilled at just the idea that he might be at the mall, might be playing in a softball game somewhere where she and MoKid could go watch.

Now he was just Bob, and she called Bob to tell him that she had Ms. Gwen Anders, and she had the lady nailed *cold.*

"What do you mean, nailed cold?" he asked. He'd been playing basketball out back, his mother said, and she'd called him in for the phone.

Kelly explained. "The fancy Ms. Gwendolyn Anders isn't who she says she is, she's living a lie."

"What do you mean a lie? *Guys, hold up.*"

"What?"

"I was talking to Tony and Mike. What do you mean she's living a lie?"

"I mean she's using a fake name—her name isn't Gwen Anders." Kelly very quickly explained about checking the college yearbook and the alumni association locator.

Bob didn't sound that impressed. "So what? That doesn't prove anything."

"What are you talking about? She said her name was Gwen Anders, she said she went to Antonmywer College."

"So maybe there's two Antonmywer colleges; maybe you just had the wrong one."

"Get real."

"Kelly, come on, think about it. She got hired as a substitute teacher; you can't just walk in off the street and do that. They must have checked on her somewhere."

Unable to believe that her alleged boyfriend didn't understand what she was trying to tell him, Kelly said, "Bob, the lady is crazy, she's lying about who she is, and the school didn't even bother to check on her."

"I don't think she's crazy."

"What?"

"I don't. She doesn't act crazy to me. At least not when I've seen her."

"She burns her fingers. She burned Creeps's fingers."

"What are you talking about?"

"I think she did, anyway." Kelly took a breath and cleared her head, and in the moment of silence

Bob asked, "You want to go down to the mall later?"

"No. I'm working on this."

"Working on what?"

"Proving that Ms. Anders is a crazy lady. She's got a thing about pain, and suicide, and I'll tell you something else—I think she killed Mrs. Hanson."

"Say *what*?"

"That's what I think."

"You haven't said this to anybody, have you?"

"No, but I'm going to."

"I don't think you better. Think about it—why would Ms. Anders have wanted to kill Mrs. Hanson? What would her motive be? She didn't even know the lady."

"I think she did it so she could take her job."

"That's nuts; a teacher's job doesn't pay enough to kill anybody over—besides, there's plenty of jobs for teachers."

"Not so many. Besides, I told you—Ms. Gwen Anders is a maniac."

"Kelly . . ." Bob started to say one thing, then seemed to change his mind and say another instead. "Be careful, Kelly."

"What do you care?"

"I care. You could get into a lot of trouble saying things like that if you can't prove anything."

"Prove anything?" said Kelly, suddenly thinking very deviously, making very spooky plans in her head. "Oh, don't worry about that. I'm going to prove *everything*. . . ."

Dear Ms. Whoever you are . . .

Kelly admired her handiwork, the typewritten words on the page that was going to send Ms. Gwen Anders—or whoever she was—screaming into the night. Especially in light of what had come to Kelly in the mail that afternoon. As she was typing it she took a break to dial the telephone.

"Operator, what city, please?"

"Long Beach," said Kelly. "Do you have a listing for Anders? It's probably new."

"I show a G. Anders on Lamont Street."

"Which number was that?"

"414 Lamont."

"That's it—could I have the number please?"

"One moment." The operator pushed some button and the recording played and Kelly jotted down the number. Then she hung up and went back to her letter. *I've got you now, Ms. Gwen Whoever,* she thought. *I've got you now. . . .*

Which is what Kelly told her friends the next day at lunch. The MoKid was suitably impressed by the research involved, but not so sure about the plan. Kelly hadn't gone into detail, certainly didn't mention Operation Torment or any of the terrible dreams she was having about Mrs. Hanson, but did tell them she planned to dig under the substitute's skin a little bit. Tara wasn't around and Janice was with Bob—they thought what she had in mind was stupid.

"Well, it's too late," said Kelly. "I already called her once."

"What?" It took Bob a minute to register that.

"I did." Kelly almost giggled from the release. "I left a message on her answering machine, and I said *I know who you are and I know what you did*."

"Kelly . . ."

"I'm sending her a letter, too. I already wrote it, and I just need to stick it in the mail."

"Why?"

"Because I want to make this lady crazy. Crazier than she already is."

Janice didn't understand. "Why?"

"Because of what she did to Mrs. Hanson."

"You don't know she did anything to Mrs. Hanson."

"I do—I know what's going on here. Look at this."

Bob and Janice both did; MoKid ignored it. "Your grade report, yeah. I got mine, too; I did all right."

"Look at my history grade."

"Yeah?"

"So she failed me in history."

"So?"

"So I never get below a B in anything."

"Yeah," said Janice, "but you never become an obsessive maniac in anything else, either."

Bob agreed.

Kelly looked at MoKid, who shrugged. Kelly shook her head, saying, explaining, "This is more proof."

"Kelly, all this proves is you didn't pay attention in class at all."

"Pay attention? I was the teacher's aide."

"You *were*. I don't know . . ."

"You don't know what?"

"I need to go see Mr. Taylor," said Janice. She gathered her stuff and left, MoKid following. Bob sat there a long moment with Kelly, waiting to say something.

The wait made her more anxious than anything; finally Kelly asked, "Why don't you guys believe what I'm telling you?"

"We never said we didn't believe you." Bob sighed, then he said, "Listen, I was thinking, all things considered, maybe we shouldn't go out for a while."

That almost made Kelly laugh—check, she *did* laugh. "You're breaking up with me?"

Another hesitation. Then: "Yeah, I think so."

Another laugh. "Well, don't think so hard. I was going to break up with you, anyway. Just go."

"Okay. Sorry." Bob got up and left the table, taking his stuff with him. Kelly sat there another long while, alone, and wondered what to do next. Send another zinger Ms. Anders's way? Really push the woman?

Why not just tell somebody who might listen? That seemed the easiest possibility. Tell the office, tell the principal, the authorities, *somebody*, and they would do whatever needed to be done. Except . . . except for what she did to Mrs. Hanson. That was different, Kelly thought.

That was personal.

When Mrs. Hanson died it was as if Kelly had slipped into a hole and then become the hole, unable to climb out from within herself and aware of hardly anything else; it surprised her to find such selfishness coming so easy. Except maybe this was what confronting death was; Kelly couldn't be sure. She had never before known anyone who died, never expected anyone she knew to die. Probably that was unrealistic, especially with her mother being a policeman, but so be it, there it was.

Then, suddenly, no warning and Mrs. H was dead, and Kelly knew who caused her to die, or at least thought she did.

No, the word was *knew*. An *absolute*. To allow any doubt into the equation would be to allow Ms. Gwen Anders the phony off the hook, and on the hook was where Kelly wanted her. On the hook and swinging like poor Mrs. Hanson, like poor Sandy—

Sandy Hanson. *Sandy*. Whenever Kelly thought of her that way, as more than her old teacher, as a lost human being, it always hurt, like a crystal bullet boring straight through the forehead and out through the back of the skull; just an aching tunnel of light.

But there she was, would be forever; hanging in Kelly's memory and in that closet, bleached pale and eyes open.

So that was why Kelly didn't talk about things, didn't pull herself so quickly from the dark hole she had become, didn't forget and certainly didn't forgive.

Mrs. Hanson was gone and wasn't coming back,

and that wasn't a concept an optimist dealt with
very well, even one so consumed with doomsdays
and various armageddons; even divorced fathers
paid the occasional courtesy call; they still loved
you. The dead were denied visitation rights, and
substitute teachers could apparently call the roll
any way they liked. . . .

On Thursday Kelly had one of the first serious
talks she'd had with Janice in a long time; try forever. Since Bob obviously wasn't eating lunch with
her anymore, it seemed an interesting distraction.
She and Janice had always been casual friends, the
extra person or pair on an excursion, someone to
confer with at lunch, not like the MoKid
or . . . well, the MoKid.

Janice had a box of caramel corn and a case of
the guilts, but she wasn't anyone's push-away; she
dropped down beside Kelly on the wall across from
the Double J auditorium building and offered Kelly
a handful of the sticky candy, which she accepted,
and chewed, and waited for it.

"Halloween's coming."

"Yeah," said Kelly. *So's* Operation Torment.
But she didn't say that.

"I wonder who's having parties? We should
have our own party, except that's never as much
fun as going out to parties. What are you going to
go as? Don't you miss trick-or-treat? Sometimes I
wish Halloween was still trick-or-treat."

Kelly didn't say anything. She was still waiting
for it.

Janice took another handful of caramel corn

from the box, chewed, and said, "You broke up with Bob, huh?"

"Yeah."

"Are you mad?"

"Huh?"

"Were you . . . I mean, you did love him, right?"

What was this? Kelly wondered. Was Janice suddenly running interference for Bob? Trying to get them back together? Kelly didn't have time for this, did she? Still . . .

Bob was all right, *wasn't he?* So they'd had a fight—over something very important, over Ms. Anders—but still . . .

"I don't know," said Kelly, not committing herself. This was something she needed to think about for a while, something she and Bob should talk about alone, not through friends.

"Well . . ." said Janice, working her way around to the subject, easing into it, "it's just that there's something."

"Something?"

"Yeah, well . . ."

Janice was blushing, her face growing red; she was embarrassed. *What?* What could Bob have possibly asked her to say?

Kelly chewed on caramel corn and waited.

Janice looked away, not meeting Kelly's eyes, when she said, all in a rush as if it was one long word, "Bob wants me to go out with him, you know, and I want to but I won't if it's going to hurt you, you don't still care for him, do you?"

"Oh, for Pete's sake."

"I'm sorry."

"*Sorry?*" Now Kelly was embarrassed, but for the life of her she couldn't think of any reason she would be, except she felt as if some part of her had been jarred loose and was clunking around on the inside, but that was stupid. *Fine*, she wanted to say, *fine, go out with him, you guys do whatever you want, who cares? I'm on a mission.*

Except she couldn't say she was on a mission, she couldn't really say anything much at all except, "Do whatever you want."

"It's okay?"

"Whatever. I . . ."

Janice waited.

Kelly stared at her. "You've got caramel corn stuck in your teeth."

It was the worst thing she could think of to say.

Before she went back to class, Kelly stopped by the pay phone and called Ms. Anders's answering machine again. Disguising her voice as best she could she taunted, saying, *"The police are on to you, Gwen Anders. They know all about what you aren't. Isn't that them pulling into your driveway now?"*

Then she hung up.

After school Kelly had the first serious talk she'd had with Doug the thug in a long time; try forever. Ma wasn't around, she was working a double shift—which could either mean a stakeout, some serious crime, or just a lot of extra paperwork piled up—and Doug had brought home a bucket of fried chicken and all the trimmings. Kelly loved chicken, but her appetite wasn't completely recovered, especially when she had to eat with Doug, but even the shock of his personality couldn't dull you forever.

"They're doing a haunted house at the main fire station," Doug said.

"They do every year," said Kelly.

"I thought you might be interested."

"I see too many scary things as it is."

"Come on, Knock-Knock, give me a break . . ."

"A break?"

"I'm sorry. I really am; I'm working at this thing. Did your mother tell you I . . . I'm in therapy, I mean."

"So what does that mean?"

"It means I'm seeing somebody."

"Terrific."

"I'm serious, I'm with somebody now and what they suggested was maybe—maybe—a lot of the problem isn't between your mother and me, but you and me, there's a tension there."

"You know what's weird?" Kelly sat back in her chair and tried to explain herself. "My favorite person—my teacher—she kills herself, except I know she didn't kill herself because I know who killed her, and it's this crazy substitute from school who isn't who she pretends to be and all of that doesn't mean anything, because compared to what I've got going on around me at home it almost seems normal."

"Kelly . . ."

"It almost seems normal."

"I'm trying to get some help for myself. I just want you to work with your mother and me on this."

"Ma does what she wants, she always has."

"Kelly . . ."

"I didn't want her to leave Dad, but I guess he was too nice to her. She hates that I guess, guys being too nice to her; I don't know why. It's like that old Groucho Marx line, I think; she doesn't want to belong to any club that would have her as a member, she doesn't want to be with anyone who likes her that much."

"It's not like that."

"That's her story, I don't know what yours is; who cares? I'm that much like Ma. We just look at the bright side and get on with things."

Doug the thug spoke with such practiced effort that he even held up his open hands in a forced gesture he must have read about in a book; *sickening.* He said, "I don't mean to take your dad's place."

"Don't worry about it." Kelly very nearly laughed. "My dad doesn't have your supercharged personality, I guess; Ma thinks my dad is a wimp but he's not. If he knew you slapped me, he'd probably kill you, but he's a nice guy and he finished last. That's the way of the world. Ma does what she wants and I can't help that, but that's between you and her; leave me out of it. If your shrink says for you to buy me fried chicken, fine, I've got to eat, but if you want forgiveness, go find yourself a priest."

Kelly was thinking of Bob when she said that,

Bob and Janice and it was appropriate, really; it was the meanest thing she could think of to say. Then she went upstairs, got changed for the evening, and called Ms. Anders on the telephone again. . . .

The next morning, before school and in a flash of brilliance, Kelly composed her own classified ad for *Impossible Detective* magazine, intended for the Investigative Column—where bounty hunters, police, and buffs exchanged information on wandering suspects and bail jumpers. The small ad cost twenty-seven dollars and would, the instructions said and Kelly was sure, make it just in time for the next published issue:

SUBSTITUTE TEACHER: Blond, blue eyes, suicidal, using alias Gwen Anders in N/W IN town of Long Beach. Many suspect relationships, possible crimes in background. Anyone with information.

She didn't have an ad ID number; the magazine said they'd forward all the responses to her. . . .

11

Monday morning, Kelly's study hall hour after history and Debi LeDonne—a fabled party animal with teased red hair and purple glasses—was sitting answering telephones, very nervous as she spoke to Kelly. "If you get caught, I'm going to get in big trouble. I need the office assistant hour for my work-study credit."

"I won't get caught, Deb. Come on."

Debi hesitated, but nodded, agreeing to look the other way while Kelly snuck around back by the files, Mr. Boughamer's files, the school personnel files. "See if there's anything neat in Mr. Smith's file—he's so *cute.*"

"Biology Smith?"

"*No*! French teacher Smith."

"I can't, I'm on a mission."

"A mission. *Right.*"

Kelly was on a mission, and the first drawer she looked in while trying to carry it out was the wrong one. PLOEN, MICHAEL, said the first file, but that wasn't even close to what she was looking for; Mike Ploen was just the landscaper, just the janitor for the grass, famous for having once been the

Double J starting quarterback in his time but now he was the dirt guy.

Interesting, but Kelly slid the drawer shut and checked the cabinet to the left. What she was looking for was third from the front.

There. ANDERS, GWEN, said the file label. Ms. Gwen Anders's personnel documents. Kelly pulled out the manila folder and flipped the file open. It was all there, Antonmywer College, previous experience with the California public and private school systems; she'd been with the Long Beach Community School System for less than a year, that was why she was subbing, trying to work her way—

Someone was in the hall.

Kelly went to return the file—*damn*. The file cabinet drawer had locked itself shut, and Kelly couldn't sit around trying to jimmy it open. *Now what?* She sat there fiddling with the latch a minute, trying to figure out how to get it back open, when a figure appeared in her path before she could hide what she was up to.

"What are you doing?"

It was Creeps. The relief at not having been nailed by one of the staff almost made her swoon. What was Creeps doing here? "I'm not doing anything," said Kelly.

He was frowning, all caught up in his responsibilities. "You aren't an office aide. What are you doing here?"

Kelly tried the best defense is a good offense trick. She answered back by asking, "What are *you* doing here?"

"Gwen sent me down to pick up some papers."

"Gwen?"

"Ms. Anders."

"I got sent for something, too."

"No . . ." Creeps shook his head. "You're supposed to be in study hall. You're ditching, and I don't know what you're doing."

"Come on, give us a break."

"What?" Creeps seemed to suddenly realize what Kelly was holding in her hands. "Those are the teachers' files."

"Yeah. Listen . . ."

"What are you doing?"

"I'm not doing anything. I'm—listen, Creeps, there's something really weird going on here. I need your help."

"My help? Why should I help you?"

"Seriously, I—"

"Forget you. I'm calling somebody."

"Creeps, come on—"

He took off, away, off to rat her out.

No way am I waiting for this, Kelly thought, and she started to pack it up quickly, but the file drawer was still locked. What was she supposed to do? Just leave the file on top of the drawer? Total evidence of what she was doing?

Leave with it? Hide it someplace?

I used to be an A student, Kelly was thinking. *Teacher's pet, hard studier, lots of activities, and now I'm a detective in a lot more trouble than a person really needs. Why me? Ma's the detective, not me. Is it in the blood?*

Take the file with you, she thought. After all, it's evidence.

No way. If it was found in her locker she was dead meat—*absolutely* dead. So Kelly did the next best thing, and stuffed it into one of the hallway trash cans during the confusion of the between class hallway muddle, then headed off to algebra, except a face appeared in the doorway, the white pasty face Kelly had been seeing in her shudders ever since getting nailed. It was Mr. Boughamer, the principal. Not just the vice principal, but the big guy himself.

"Go ahead, Kelly," said Mrs. Stephenson, and Kelly nodded, taking her books and things and following Mr. B down the hall, down the stairs, and into the admin office.

Resigned, she followed him back into the office, past Tara—who was working the desk now and wisely choosing to ignore her—and into Boughamer's inner office, where the first face she saw was Ms. Gwen Anders. And the substitute was *trembling. . . .*

Despite her edge on the bright side, Kelly's world used to end all the time; as with most of her doomsdays she never had a chance in Mr. Boughamer's office.

They wouldn't see it that way, of course; they would, of course, say they gave Kelly every chance—Ms. Anders hadn't jumped all over Kelly; she seemed too upset herself. "Kelly," she said, weakly, not the strong lady from class. "Kelly, we need to talk."

"Yeah," agreed Kelly. "We sure do."

"We're all going to talk," said Mr. Boughamer, who was still standing, and pointed Kelly to a seat. From his desk he held up a small black cassette tape. "This is from Ms. Anders's telephone answering machine, Kelly. Care to venture a guess as to whose voice is on it?"

"I know whose voice is on it," said Kelly. "Mine."

"Kelly . . ."

Ms. Anders cleared her throat. "Mr. Boughamer, could I talk to Kelly alone for just a moment."

"Absolutely," said the principal. "I just talked to Kenny Newlan and I need to check something out anyway."

Creeps ratted her out. Oh, well, what did she expect? The evidence was long gone, anyway.

Mr. B left them alone together and Kelly saw that Ms. Anders was genuinely frightened of her; the substitute actually had tears welling up in her eyes. "Why?" she asked. "I won't . . . I won't ask you how you know whatever you know, but *why*?"

Kelly actually felt a rush of power, of *control*. She had control over the substitute now, here in the principal's office and she, Kelly, was in *control*. Of course she was; she knew the substitute's dirty secrets. "Why? You know why, because of what you did to Sandy."

"Who?"

"Mrs. Hanson."

"I swear, Kelly, I didn't do anything to Mrs. Hanson."

So pathetic, Kelly thought, *so pathetic*. "You're the suicide expert, aren't you?"

"Kelly . . ."

"What about Antonmywer College? You didn't go there, I checked."

The substitute's face was very reasoned, very calm. "Listen to me, please."

"Gwen Anders is dead. Who are you?"

"I *am* Gwen Anders. I did go to Antonmywer."

"Not according to the alumni association. They've got a locator service—you didn't know that, did you?"

"I did—I do—Kelly, *please*—"

"I know all about you, lady, all about you—"

"*Please*, stop doing this to me."

"I haven't even started what I'm going to do to you, *killer*."

"What?"

"You're a *killer*."

"No. Kelly, *listen* to me—"

"I don't have to listen to you."

"There's things you don't know. I've just been trying to get my life back together, Kelly."

"Well, you came to the wrong place to do it. I'm not like my ma, Ms. Gwen Anders or whoever you really are—I don't let the bad guys win."

"Bad guys." The substitute nodded, wiping at the dampness of her eyes, but suddenly they weren't damp, they were cold, ice-cold. Nice to ice; like before. "Don't mess with me, Kelly Wallis. I'm tougher than you think."

"I know. I've seen you making yourself tougher. How's your fingers?"

The substitute had no opportunity to answer that one, because Mr. Boughamer returned then, carrying a small shoe box; he looked a little pale. Ms. Anders addressed him, saying, "I'm afraid Kelly and I have never properly gotten on, especially in light of . . . what happened to Mrs. Hanson."

"We all know what happened to Mrs. Hanson," said Kelly.

"Quite. All things considered, Mr. Boughamer, I was thinking that it might perhaps be better for all concerned if Kelly was perhaps moved to another history class."

That made Kelly snort a laugh. "You're kicking me out of your class? *You?*"

"I think we have a bigger problem than that, Ms. Anders," said Mr. Boughamer, which irritated Kelly. Mr. Boughamer was suddenly Doug the thug, explaining to her in no uncertain terms why he got to make the rules and people like Ma and Mrs. Hanson got to be run over by the Gwen Anderses and Doug the thugs of the world. *No way.*

"We sure do," said Kelly. "The problem is this lady is a murdering maniac."

"*Quiet,*" said Mr. B, upset but trying to remain professional, trying to stress his training over whatever his gut reaction might right now be. "Ms. Wallis, we've crossed some lines here."

They found the file in the trash. *Damn.*

Except it wasn't the file, couldn't be, because Mr. B said, "I've just come from your locker, Kelly."

"You went in my locker?"

"I have that right."

Kelly nodded, speaking in a quieter tone now. "Well, everything in there's mine. No problem."

"There's a big problem, Kelly."

"What?"

"What's in this box."

Ms. Anders looked first, immediately choked and backed away. "*Oh my God.*"

Kelly looked inside, instantly gagged.

There was a dead animal in the box; a cat, a grey-and-black kitten tabby, strangled, its neck wrung. Motionless, it lay on the bottom of the shoe box, sprawled like a hand puppet with no hand inside, its eyes wide open and as empty as glass with nothing behind them.

"This *atrocity* was in your locker, young lady." Mr. B was barely containing himself, shuddering.

"I . . . I . . ." Kelly couldn't speak, certainly couldn't look at that *thing*. "I swear I didn't . . ."

"Where did you get this horror, Kelly? What were you going to do with it? *Whose cat is this?*"

Ms. Anders answered that one, tears welling in her eyes. "That's my kitten, Mr. Boughamer. She killed my baby kitten. . . ."

Detective Phil Edgar was the one who picked Kelly up from school, and at first it seemed innocent enough. He was a frequent partner of Ma's, a friend, and seemed surprised to be called down to the school, and defensive of Kelly. "We'll look into *everything*," was all he kept saying.

Kelly was definitely glad to see him. Of all the people who might have shown up at the school—including Ma and Doug the thug—Edgar was probably the mellowest. She'd known him for years, even had a minor crush on him when they first got to town. Detective Edgar was just a little younger than Ma, had curly brown hair, and a neatly trimmed mustache which always seemed to be right over a smile. Kelly waited in the outer office a minute while he finished up with Mr. Boughamer, and then he walked her out.

When they went out to his car, Kelly almost relaxed; it was definitely good to be away from Mr. Boughamer's office, all the horrible stuff in there. "Where's Ma?" she asked Edgar.

"South Bend," he said. "She was driving over an extradition, her and Landy. They won't be back until this evening."

"Are you going to take me home?"

"Yeah. I need to swing by the station first. Is that okay?"

"Whatever," said Kelly, feeling as if the strength was completely sapped from her body. "I'm just glad to be out of there."

"That'll work." They drove downtown to the new police building—it wasn't but a block from the library; Kelly walked by it often enough. "Want to come in?" he asked.

"I can wait here."

"Nah, come on in. It's getting too cold for that; besides, I'm not sure how long this'll take. Come on in and I'll buy you a Coke."

"Okay." Kelly followed him in and up the stairs. They were buzzed in past security and Kelly saw the familiar rows of cluttered desks and half-eaten lunches and soda cans, back to the station Edgar worked out of. "Grab a sit-down," he said, moving as if to get some work from the big pile in his IN basket. Then he looked up. "Hey, while you're here, let me ask you something."

"What?"

"Sit down." Edgar gestured and Kelly finally did; he settled behind the desk himself. "This is some crazy stuff from school, isn't it?"

"Yeah. It's that substitute."

"Oh yeah?"

"Yeah," said Kelly, wondering if she should try and explain the whole story, go back to the beginning and lay it on him. He only seemed to be half-listening.

"You got a beef with this substitute?"

106

"Yeah. I think so."

"Because she fired you from that . . . *what's it?* Class aide? Why would you care about that?"

Kelly tried to be both calm and serious before the discussion got out of her control; she was beginning to realize she had been tricked into all of this. "It's not that."

"You didn't kill her cat, did you?"

"I didn't even know she *had* a cat."

The big detective nodded, then asked, "How did it wind up in your locker, do you think?"

"Somebody put it there. She put it there, I'll bet. Probably wasn't even her cat, just one she picked up somewhere."

Edgar shook his head. "Uh-uh. Came from one of the other teachers, her cat had a litter. Mrs. O'Reilly? You know her?"

Algebra Two O'Reilly. Yeah, Kelly knew her.

"This other teacher lady says Ms. Anders has had that cat for almost a month."

"So?"

"So it doesn't seem real likely that she'd kill her own kitten and stuff it into your locker, does it?"

"It seems likely to me. The lady is crazy."

"Why do you think she's crazy?"

"Lots of reasons. She—"

"What about *this*," asked Edgar.

Kelly felt nervous for a moment, because now Detective Edgar was pushing forward a familiar-looking notebook, MoKid's gift to her from the pages of *Impossible Detective* magazine. It was the *Operation Torment* plan.

Feeling weak and betrayed, Kelly said, "That . . . that was a game."

"A game?" Edgar was flipping through the pages and clippings now. There was a lot of stuff there; it had seemed funny and excessive even when MoKid put it together.

"It's from a long time ago," Kelly said.

"This was in your locker along with the cat in the box. This is like a notebook about revenge, right?"

Kelly didn't say anything.

"Revenge and retribution, it says. Pretty grisly stuff in here."

"I know."

"How much of this stuff did you do to that poor lady, Kelly?"

"She's not a poor lady."

"We know about the calls and the letters and—"

"*She's not a poor lady!*"

Detective Edgar stopped flipping pages, staring calmly into Kelly's eyes. "Kelly, there's a bit in this revenge notebook about killing people's pets. Did you kill that woman's cat, Kelly?"

"No, I didn't."

"Does your mother know about how you feel about this lady?"

Edgar was *enjoying* this, Kelly realized with a flash of horror, and an instant later she realized why. She always thought of Edgar and the other detectives as being Ma's partners, but they were also her *competitors*, all working toward the same merit raises, the same promotions. It was so obvious—smear Kelly, it was the same thing as smearing Ma. They could bring Ma down.

And Kelly was helping them.

Oh, no. . . .

"Hey, Phil? Got a minute?" A voice from the captain's office was yelling and Detective Edgar shifted his attention.

"I'm sorry," Edgar said to Kelly, rising to walk toward the back of the offices.

Ma wasn't going to be there for hours. What was going to happen in the meantime? Was she just going to be formally arrested, booked? *Photographed?* This was crazy, she didn't do anything, all she did was try to solve a puzzle, a suspicious riddle, a crazy lady teaching school who wasn't anything that she said she was.

Kelly knew she needed to act fast. *Now.* Lifting some files from Edgar's desk, Kelly rose and walked calmly—very calmly—toward the door. The exit, she knew, led downstairs to the copy room in the basement, and forward to the front door.

The only question was honesty; had Edgar been telling the truth when he said he'd made no big thing of anything yet? Did anyone know she was the number one suspect in a cat murder?

Steady breathing. Take it in, *one-two, one-two*.

Mrs. Jazzner was working the desk and the buzzer which freed open the door; she smiled at Kelly. "Haven't seen you around in a while."

"No," said Kelly, forcing a smile of her own. She held up the folders, saying, "Need to make some copies."

Mrs. J pressed the hidden buzzer, clicking open the exit door and allowing her out.

Kelly left the folders atop the trash can in the hall and got out of the building as quick as she could, running down the hall and the stairs; the closest exit was through the parking garage, and as she ran that way she passed a couple of TV camera monitors; she didn't bother to hide her face.

Was she escaping from jail now? *What the hell was she doing?*

Not much. As it was Kelly got no farther than the parking garage before Detective Edgar caught up with her, a little out of breath from the run. "Kelly!" he yelled, before she could get out of the hollow-sounding garage. She could have bolted, but again all the strength slipped right out of her. Edgar jogged over. "Hey," he said. "Easy, *easy.* What are you taking off for?"

"Because you think I'm the one who's sick."

"I don't think anything, Kelly, I'm just asking a few questions."

"Right."

"Come on, give me a break. It's not like you're under arrest or anything—it was only a cat. We'll get to the bottom of this, come on back up. I can't let you just walk, you were suspended from school, remember. Let's call your stepfather to come get you."

"Okay." Kelly followed him back upstairs. What choice did she have?

Suspended.
Kelly had never seen a suspension slip in her

110

life, but she was looking at one when Doug the thug arrived to pick her up at the police station; Detective Edgar released her into his custody without so much as a signed document.

Doug, of course, thought this was the perfect opportunity for him. Not to chew her up and spit her out, but to have the loving, consoling stepfather moment she wasn't about to allow him. "Look, you picked me up but I don't have to ride home with you."

"You're going home."

"Not with you."

"Fine." Doug slammed on the Jeep's brakes and sneered; they'd only driven a few blocks. "Go on, Knock-Knock, get out if you're going to—I had plans for the rest of the day myself."

So Kelly walked, and she walked for a long while, which wasn't the great idea it had seemed at first because her knee started to hurt again— probably time for another trip to the doctor to see if it was time for yet another cut-and-paste experiment. There was a wonderful thought.

Appropriate for the day, though. Up high and above the sky was clouding up; probably going to rain again. . . .

She came across Tyrone Tanner outside of the Dairy Queen; whether he was suspended as well, or simply ditching school, she didn't know. Unlike Kelly, Tyrone had a driver's license and he was parked, sitting on the hood of his old Pontiac, watching her as she walked over. Kelly would never have gone near excepting that Tyrone was alone for once, save for the attentions of the carhop; he was eating from a small sundae cup and watching her as she approached. What was she going to do? Run off?

Tyrone's eyes were always dark, haunted, as if denied sleep for a long time. He was a lot taller than Kelly, and she had to look up to talk to him as he held court on his car. "What's up?" he asked.

"Not enough," she answered, trying to think of something to say. Remembering something from class earlier in the year, back when Mrs. Hanson was still there, and things were still fun, she asked him, "Is your middle name really Tiberius?"

"You remember that, huh?" He seemed amused. "Tyrone Tiberius Tanner. Think of me as T.T., but don't ever call me that."

"Why not?"

"Well, there's two other T.T. Tanners in my family tree; one was a lieutenant colonel caught up in the American revolutionary war—fighting for the British. The other was a cavalry officer during the Civil War, fighting for the South. Being the third guy in the family to wake up with the name T.T. Tanner, my ambition is never to face any important choices, such as deciding which side to ally with in a war."

"So what happened between you and Ms. Anders?"

"Why do you care?"

"Because I think she's crazy."

There was a long, quiet pause, and then Tyrone nodded, saying, "Yeah, I'd say you're right about that one."

"You would? Really?"

"Absolutely."

"Why?"

"What do you mean why?"

"I don't know—I mean, I know what *I* know. What do you know?"

"I don't know anything."

"So what do you think?"

Staring hard into Kelly's eyes a long moment, Tyrone finally crawled down from the hood of his car and said, "I don't really need this going all over the known universe."

"I won't tell anyone."

"Sure."

"I swear."

Tyrone nodded, but didn't answer. Instead he

said, "You want to go to Klepp's Arcade with me?"

"What?"

"Ride down to the arcade with me and I'll tell you about me and the sub."

"I . . . I'm going with somebody," Kelly said automatically.

"That's not what I hear."

Kelly blushed. Then she got mad, but before she could do anything else Tyrone shrugged her off. "Fine," he said, climbing into his car.

"Wait, wait," Kelly said, just wanting to hold him up long enough to think. "Why the arcade?"

"Place to go. I figured you might like it. No big deal."

Kelly considered it. She's wasn't big on arcades or malls or whatever, but she knew Melissa the MoKid hung out down there a lot. School was just about out; maybe Melissa'd show up there. Either way, it probably wasn't dangerous or anything; Tyrone seemed less dangerous and more interesting the more you stood near him. So what did it mean if she wanted to stand near him for a little while longer? It didn't mean anything. "You'll tell me about Ms. Anders?"

"Sure. On the ride down."

Kelly got in the car.

On the ride down Tyrone did tell a story. "That Gwen Anders, she's a babe all right but she's bizarro."

"Bizarro?"

"Nuts, totally gone."

"Why? What?"

"She kissed me once. We were just talking and she leaned over and kissed me—I let her. Sure, I thought, way cool, but then she started talking about weird stuff. You know she wanted to burn me with a cigarette lighter?"

"Oh my God."

"Yeah. She's nuts."

"Did you tell anyone?"

"No. And you better not either."

"What is that supposed to mean?"

"I guess it means I don't appreciate cops as much as you do."

Kelly was actually surprised. "Meaning my mother?"

"I didn't tell my old lady, you better not tell yours."

"I won't, I won't. Don't worry." Frowning, Kelly said, "I don't appreciate the cops as much as you might think." *Especially not now*.

Tyrone seemed very serious, though; his eyes even darker than before. Kelly wanted to respond, but for an instant felt herself lost in those dark eyes, and the wicked way he wrapped one corner of his lip in a twisted smile. "Life'll beat us down," he said. "Life'll beat us down if we let it."

"Not me," said Kelly.

The funny thing was, Kelly was almost disappointed when Melissa the MoKid did show up at the arcade, and linking up with her wasn't especially difficult since Tyrone disappeared off with his own friends; Kelly almost felt hurt. Why? All she'd wanted was information, right? This wasn't a date, it was an interrogation, right?

Right?

Melissa the MoKid had problems of her own. Her dog, a mutt chow named Shannon, had puppies every fall, just like clockwork; every year Kelly helped find homes for the puppies of the litter. This task especially bothered Kelly since she badly wanted a dog of her own, but Doug hated dogs and Ma left the decision to him.

It was enough to make a person crazy.

So the MoKid was distracted, running puppy calculations through her head, trying to remember which of her friends had dogs and which did not. Kelly was trying to find out what happened at school after she left, but MoKid was more concerned with what had happened to her.

"They took me to jail, then they let me out."

"Jail?"

"They just asked questions; they think I killed the substitute's cat. She killed her own cat."

"What?"

"I know she did."

"You didn't start *Operation Torment*."

"I did," Kelly admitted. "But I didn't go that far."

"Would you?"

"What?"

"Would you go that far?"

"No," said Kelly, but then that voice was in her head again. *Not even for Mrs. Hanson?*

"What about Bob?" asked MoKid.

"Bob? *Forget* about Bob."

"Right."

Leaving the mall, they went to the MoKid's house to see the puppies; Kelly hadn't been there in a while, and on the way they talked about Operation Torment. "I meant that for Doug the thug," MoKid was saying.

"The substitute is a murderer," Kelly declared, although MoKid still seemed unconvinced. It didn't matter. "I can prove it. I'm going to prove it."

MoKid's dad sold insurance, and he was really into actuaries, figures, and statistics, and was forever quoting the odds of certain things happening. "It ain't in the cards, kid." That was one of his lines. "On the other hand, anything's possible. Lloyd's of London makes a terrific amount of money letting people insure themselves against meteor strikes, Martian invasions, sea monster attacks, other crazy things."

"What about homicidal maniacs subbing in your history class?" asked Kelly.

"Ain't in the cards, kid. Ain't in the cards."

Kelly didn't stay for dinner at MoKid's, not with all the which-way going on the stuff she still planned to lay on Ms. Anders via her answering machine and another letter she had yet to mail. She went home, but was met practically at the door by Ma, who hadn't even taken off her shoulder holster yet; she looked every bit a detective right out of the movies, a little tense, a little sweaty, more anxious than she had any reason to be; except at this moment Kelly suddenly remembered everything she had been trying to forget about the day.

Damn. Suspended and probably grounded, too.

"Where were you?" Ma was angry, so be it.

"I needed to take a walk."

"A walk."

"Yeah."

"Where were you, Kelly?"

"Around." Kelly considered this, and said, "I just needed to be away. I've got a problem."

"I know about your problem. I've got one, too."

"I know. I'm sorry. . . ."

"I need to know where you were today, Kelly. I know about the phone calls you've been making. And the threats."

"I know, but there's a reason—"

"A *reason*?"

"Yeah, I—"

"My gun is missing, Kelly. The Beretta from the bedroom? The one you pointed at Doug. Do you have any idea where it is now?"

Oh my God. "What do you mean it's missing?"

"Where's my gun, Kelly? What have you done with the gun?"

"I haven't done anything with the gun," said Kelly, snapping totally alert, her blood a little bit chilled by the implication. "I swear, I haven't touched it since."

Ma waited, saying nothing. Maybe she believed Kelly, maybe she didn't. She didn't pace, but stood waiting for more. Down the hall Doug the thug was getting ready for work; he had the night shift for a while.

Working up the energy, Kelly slipped off her jacket and said, "Let me tell you what I know about the substitute." She explained the phone call she had made to the Antonmywer alumni association, the answers she received, and the research she'd done on Ms. Gwen Anders, although she didn't say anything about placing the ad in *Impossible Detective*. Kelly just wanted the important things out for discussion. "The woman's a fake, Ma. A fake what, I don't know."

"A lot of people use fake names, Kelly. Or change them, legally."

"It's not legal to use someone else's name, though."

"No, it's not. But there's no real proof of that."

"But you could get proof, right?"

"Maybe. If there's anything to find."

"There's stuff to find, I swear."

Doug the thug was leaving now, and he took the opportunity to make a sarcastic crack. "That a girl, Knock-Knock. Stick to your guns." Doug cackled and pulled the door closed behind him.

"This is nuts," said Kelly.

Ma was grim. "You're beginning to frighten me, Kelly."

"I don't know anything," Kelly said, her head starting to pound, her eyes feeling like wet gobs; she suddenly realized she was almost weak from hunger. The cookie she had nibbled at the mall had done nothing to alleviate her appetite. "Can I get something to eat?"

"Yeah," said Ma, easing some. They went out to the kitchen and tossed together some dinner, Kelly catching the occasional glance from Ma, the unasked questions flipping across Kelly's brain like wet bed sheets in the wind.

"Look," said Ma. "If I said I'd look into all of this substitute thing, would you just tell me what you've done with the gun?"

"I haven't touched the gun—why would I?"

"You just might because of this substitute thing." Ma was very thoughtful, very police thoughtful. "I mean, if you're so convinced that she's some sort of a dangerous criminal who's out to get you, who's to say what you might do?"

The conversation was very much like the one she and Detective Edgar had had, and that outraged

Kelly. "I didn't do anything with the gun. I didn't touch the gun, I already told you that."

"Fine."

"You believe me?"

"The gun is missing, Kelly, and I believe you know something you're not telling. I'm sorry."

"No, you're not sorry," said Kelly. "You're a cop. . . ."

Lying on her back in bed, Kelly stared at the ceiling tiles and listened to the weather outside deteriorate; another fall thunderstorm brewing. So wonderful. There was a stack of homework over on her desk—the school system thoughtfully levied such a requirement on kids who were suspended, just to ensure they weren't getting free days off—and Kelly considered working on it, but then she changed her mind. Better to contemplate the rain.

Had she a phone in her room she might have called MoKid, or anybody, but she didn't, and besides, what was she likely to say, anyway?

So be it. Just another minor doomsday. Builds character.

Kelly started to go back downstairs at one point, but heard Ma in the kitchen on the telephone; she was talking to Dad, Kelly's father. It had been a while since the two of them had a conversation, and now Ma was all huddled concern. Kelly listened for a minute, long enough to hear the main jist of the conversation; Ma's side, anyway. She wasn't happy. "I told you what I'm going to do about it, I just want to know if you'll pay half.

"Jim, she's your daughter, too . . .

"Jim . . ."

"Fine. Whatever. You don't understand the sort of strain she's under—you grew up in a regular home. Yeah, a real regular home. I just need to know if you'll pay half. Fine, do whatever you want. *Whatever.*

"Good-bye."

The next day was blah. It started early enough, with Kelly up and dressed before she remembered being suspended and that took the rush off of everything. Ma was early on the telephone again, but Kelly couldn't easily tell with whom and couldn't hang around eavesdropping.

Operation Torment seemed to be on hold, so Kelly sat back on her bed and stared at the ceiling another long while, but it was no longer raining outside, which was good; her knee bothered her a lot more when the weather was damp, storms threatening.

"Come on," said Ma when she appeared without warning in the doorway. "Up. Let's go."

"Where are we going?"

"You've got an appointment."

Kelly assumed that to mean something to do with the school, but that proved wrong. They went down to the medical group building and—after a few embarrassing moments in two different waiting rooms—Kelly found herself being put, alone, through the office door of MARIAN L. KENNEDY, JUVENILE PSYCHOLOGIST.

Juvenile Psychologist; wasn't that something for working with juvenile delinquents?

Psychologist. Wasn't that something close to what Mrs. Hanson had wanted to get into?

Banish that thought.

Kelly heard the door behind her clink shut and she approached the smiling woman at the big desk; the carpet was thick and soft beneath Kelly's step and there were two bubbling fish tanks in the room. "Are you supposed to straighten me out?"

"I don't do much straightening," said the counselor, a rail-thin woman with wide plastic-framed spectacles and a pointed nose; she wore a purple blouse with a colorful neckerchief, lots of red and yellow in it. She had the voice of an algebra teacher confidently reading the answers from the cheat page at the back of her textbook. "I thought we could talk a few minutes."

"A few minutes. You're a psychologist."

"A counselor, mostly."

"So don't you get paid by the hour?"

"Sometimes."

"So we talk for an hour, right?"

"Fifty-five minutes now." The woman was not about to be put in her place.

This, at least, Kelly could accept. "All right, then."

Taking the seat that was offered across from the counselor's desk—and staying as far away from the leather couch as possible—Kelly listened as the woman consulted the file on her desk and lifted a heavy-looking pen. "Can I ask you some questions? They've said some awful things about you."

"I bet they have."

"You have problems at school."

"I have one problem at school."

"Which is?"

"Didn't they tell you?"

The counselor shrugged. "I wanted to hear it from you—in case what I heard was wrong."

Again Kelly nodded. "My problem is that my substitute teacher in American history is a homicidal maniac, I can prove it, and nobody wants to hear what I say."

"Nobody wants to hear you?"

"Not for a long while."

"Ahhhh . . ."

"There's no ahhh," said Kelly, sitting up, not wanting to wind up caught in some pseudopsychiatric analysis of her life. "I'm talking about a very specific thing."

"Your parents are divorced."

"Yeah. That doesn't have anything to do with this."

"I'm sure it doesn't, but it does help with the background. I'm not trying to read so much into this as you think, Kelly; I'm just trying to get to know you."

"The problem is the substitute."

"You feel she's out to get you?"

Kelly considered this; that wasn't necessarily true. "No, not me. She does weird things, and it started with me."

"You were dismissed as a classroom aide."

"I said it started with me."

There was a moment's contemplation from the counselor on that. "And your favorite teacher killed herself. I can see how that would be upsetting."

"She didn't kill herself." Taking a breath and working up the energy, Kelly did her best to recount the tale of the substitute, starting with her first appearance at the front of Mrs. Hanson's classroom and ending with the horrible scene in Boughamer's office. The counselor took notes throughout.

"It's not me," Kelly finished up, sounding more desperate and defensive than she had intended. Way more than she had intended.

Along with Kelly's story, the hour was winding down and the counselor nodded again; the nods from this lady were becoming insufferable. If she didn't believe Kelly, why didn't she just up and call her a liar? She didn't do that, of course. What she did was change the subject, drag it back to an irrelevancy. "How long have your parents been separated?"

"They're not separated, they're divorced, and it doesn't matter."

Another nod. "When was the last time you handled your mother's gun, Kelly?"

"I don't have the gun. I didn't touch the gun."

"What about animals? Did you hurt the cat, Kelly?"

"I never hurt anything in my life."

"Well," said the counselor, nodding her final irritating nod of the morning. "At least I think it's time to get you back to school. It'll do you good to be back at school. . . ."

*　　*　　*

Maybe so, maybe not. There was a substitute for the substitute in American history Kelly's first morning back—no one had actually gone to the trouble of transferring her yet, although she expected it was only a matter of a few pieces of paper changing hands. Settled at her desk, Kelly watched with horrid fascination as the guy—it was an elderly man this time—thumbed through the thick textbook, seemingly unaware of anything that was going on.

Come on, Kelly was thinking. *This isn't just a class, this is an active corner of the universe and there is madness dwelling here.* All eyes were on her, Kelly knew; rumor control at Double J was out of hand. Kelly was both the victim and the bad guy, the girl who killed the substitute's cat and the one who got ratted out by Creeps. She was the one who drove off the substitute Gwen Anders, and only Tyrone Tanner gave her the same smile as always; he even borrowed a pencil and a sheet of paper. Kelly was grateful for the gesture, although she was so nervous that her hands almost shook as she passed the things back.

After school Kelly caught another ride to the zoo, although Tara seemed hesitant to take her. "Don't you need to be getting home or something? I know you're . . ."

"I didn't do anything," Kelly said. Tara didn't act like she believed that; they didn't say much to each other on the ride down.

Creeps was nowhere to be seen. Kelly actually looked around for him, lingered around the tiger habitat on the chance he might wander by. *Why?* Did she want to hound him for his betrayal? Kelly didn't think so. She had questions she needed answered, though.

It was in the shadows behind the small ape area, where the chimpanzees hooted and teased one another, that the substitute struck. Kelly was pulled violently off of the footpath by urgent hands and pushed down—hard—onto the cinder chip ground; if she hadn't been wearing her heavy jacket, she'd have been banged up some. Instead, she was knocked down, out of sight, with the tall form of Ms. Anders glaring coldly from above. Kelly tried to spring back, but the substitute knew some sort of martial art or something and she moved so quickly, slapping with a backhand and moving a foot to toss Kelly off balance again.

Then she pointed. "You."

"Hey!" Kelly started to yell, "Hey, I—"

Another slap—the sub's fingernails raked Kelly's cheek, but it was her words which shut Kelly up. "Stay out of my life, out of my business."

From the ground Kelly snorted. If this wasn't proof of just what this crazy lady was, she didn't know what would be. "You're too late, lady; I've already set the world loose on you."

"You don't know anything about the world."

"I know enough about *your* world. I know who you are, where you don't come from."

"Is that a fact?"

"It is."

"Well, wonderful, so very wonderful." The sub

seemed contemplative a moment, more and more bitter. "So why not tell it all to your personal head psychiatrist—and, yeah, I heard about that—as she tries and figure out why you're devoting so much attention to driving me mad."

Kelly swallowed at that. Waited.

The substitute nodded. "Life tastes like ashes in your mouth right now, young Kelly. I'm familiar with that taste. But many things burn worse."

"Like your brands? The burns you like to give people?"

"You don't even understand that. Those are our marks. You have to share a mark. Pain has to be shared for it to be bearable, Kelly. I thought you of all people might realize that."

"Meaning?"

"I should think that was obvious. Your mother the clever police lady has her pain, and her heavy-handed lover his. They beat on each other, they share each other's pain, and bear it. You're simply a burden who won't share."

"Like you shared with Mrs. Hanson."

"I didn't do anything with your teacher, Kelly. I'm just trying to survive."

"Some survival."

"Listen to me, you little . . ." Ms. Gwen Anders the substitute started to erupt, then controlled herself and spoke very calmly, full of icy reserve. "Allow me to educate you about the world," said the substitute. "If you want to make it in the real world, you need to be willing to suffer. I am—are you?"

"What?"

128

"I killed that kitten. It was my baby cat, but I took that trusting little kitten into my arms, and twisted its neck until it broke and shoved it into a box and into your locker and I *loved* that cat." Ms. Anders glared. "*You*, I don't even *like*...."

From *Impossible Detective* magazine, November issue, page 178, classified section, Investigative Column:

> *SUBSTITUTE TEACHER:* Blond, blue eyes, suicidal, using alias Gwen Anderz in N/W IN town of Long Beach. Many suspect relations, possible crimes in background. Anyone with information. Reward! Detect #441-97-254.

There was a typo in the spelling of the substitute's name, and Kelly had no reward to offer, but all in all she thought, *terrific.* . . .

Kelly tried to call her father in Chicago.

She and her father weren't exactly close, not so close as many divorced fathers seemed to be with their children, although they did share the occasional weekend and his infrequent visits to Long Beach to take her someplace; shopping, usually. Her father was a lawyer specializing in bankruptcy; he was the one who first tagged her Knock-Knock, so many years ago.

Except he wasn't home, and Linda, his current live-in girlfriend, answered and tried her best to get Kelly into a friendly, so-called spontaneous conversation, although it was obvious to Kelly that if Ma filled Dad in, he no doubt briefed Linda. "So when are you going to come see us?" she asked. "Spend the weekend; I'll take you shopping. You could bring a friend if you want, there's plenty of room."

Plenty of room? Was there enough room for Kelly to disappear herself into and never come back? Probably there was, but Kelly didn't allow herself to get caught up.

The new *Impossible Detective* magazine had

been out for a while; that was a good thing, anyway. When she felt down about things she pulled her copy from the desk and flipped through it; the ad seemed to jump right out at Kelly as she opened to the Investigative section of the classified ads in back. She couldn't help but smugly stare at it—*there you have it, ladies and gentlemen, the eventual downfall of Ms. Gwen Anders, the substitute*.

At lunch, Kelly sat watching Bob and Janice giggle together across the cafeteria, unsure as to how she felt about it. A little bad, sure, but not exactly sick. Tara was neutral—feuding with the Cohen twins—but MoKid remained loyal, sitting close and very concerned about the scratches Kelly hadn't even bothered to try and cover with makeup.

"Is that from the thug?" she asked.

"No." Kelly was eating very dry french fries, one by one, very mechanically. They had no taste.

"What happened?"

"You know what happened."

"You didn't tell me."

"Gwen Anders did it to me."

MoKid hesitated a moment. "Really?"

"Very much really. At the zoo. I was looking for Creeps."

"Why Creeps?"

"I'm on a mission."

MoKid hesitated another moment, her eyes wary. "I thought you were done with that mission."

Kelly had a strange realization. The only one who would buy into all of this, who would help her would be Gwen Anders; why couldn't they be friends, put all of this behind them, start over? It was a wild, grotesque thought, and when it was gone she very nearly blushed, as if the lunacy of that idea was what marked her face instead of the scratches.

So Kelly blinked. "Don't you believe me?"

"I don't know. It does seem kind of unlikely."

"So where's the sub these days?"

"They say she isn't feeling well."

"I hope not; I used a lot of Operation Torment working at it."

"Kelly . . ."

"I put an ad in *Impossible Detective*."

"Really?"

"*Really*. That ought to bring something out of the woodwork."

"Only if there's something in the woodwork, Kelly; only if there's something in the woodwork . . ."

That afternoon Kelly found answers to some of the questions.

Creeps wasn't in school anymore, hadn't been since the day of Kelly's return, and she had taken it on herself to track him down, although that hadn't been easy; she had to do her best to think as her mother would, at a time when she and her mother weren't getting along all that well. First she tried the comic book stores, then a few of the war-gaming clubs—the Dungeons & Dragons crowd that hung out at the public library—then, finally—on a hunch—down at the Dunes Cinema the Friday afternoon before Halloween—a new slasher movie was opening.

The Revenge Maniac was the name of the thing; the poster showed a razor-tipped claw glove slicing through the very paper of the display, although most of them did these days. The gimmick for the movie was some weird bit of nonsense called 4-D, whatever that was, and the fact that every showing of the film supposedly had a different ending; different people died. Creeps had been waiting a long time for this one, and Kelly knew it; she figured out about what time the last matinee of the afternoon would be ending, and surprised Creeps coming out. At first he stepped smartly away, but she chased after him, calling: "Creeps, *wait.*"

He did, seeming to sag under the weight of his name; she caught up at the edge of the parking lot. The sun was low and dimming in the sky; it was after five, getting colder fast. Creeps's breath blew out in a puff as he said, "What?"

"I need your help."

"My help? What with?"

"Ms. Anders, the substitute."

"The substitute?" Creeps gave out a little bit of a snort and shoved his hands in his pockets. "Go away."

"This is important."

Already he was shaking his head. "Oh, right, I'm supposed to listen to you because you're one of those bright and shiny cheerleader types from class, always with the answers. Well, what about me?"

"You?"

"I'm not going to help you attack Gwen."

"Creeps, come on. Don't you understand what she's doing? She's using you."

"Using me? Everybody uses me." Creeps walked, forcing Kelly to follow; he was ranting as he jogged across the street to the mall parking lot, and walking across the lot to the mall doors. "Need some help on a computer question, ask Creeps. Need to borrow a pencil, or a pen, or some paper, or a book, ask Creeps. Some girl needs to borrow lunch money, ask Creeps; some guy needs trig answers, ask Creeps. Don't get special on me, Kelly Knock-Knock or whatever you get called—*everybody* uses me."

"Yeah, but she's weird—"

"Weird? What do you mean? Because she likes *me*?"

"No—"

"Yeah. *Sheesh.*" Creeps almost looked as if he was going to cry; his eyes suddenly seemed like heavy bags. "Gwen likes me, she really likes me. Not like you guys. She's pretty, and smart, and I do things for her, and she *likes* me. I don't have to feel like the big class geek because I like movies and stuff nobody else does—because she likes them, too."

"She does?" That opened up some possibilities.

Creeps was still quivering. "Yeah, she likes all these movies. Chain saws and blood and stuff."

"She does." Kelly said it again. "Is that why you turned me over to Boughamer?"

Creeps was defensive. "I'm a Lictor," he said.

135

"A what?" *What was he talking about?*

"A *Lictor*. Gwen told me about them—they were officer aides to Roman *Praetors*." Creeps said this, although it was obvious he didn't understand what a Praetor was; Kelly didn't either. Probably some kind of army leader or general. Creeps said, "The Lictor bore the Fasces as the insignia of his office."

"His office?"

"*My* office. The Lictor clears the way, enforces respect for his superior, arresting offenders."

"Like you did with me."

Creeps ignored that. He said, "He also executes the condemned."

Kelly swallowed. "Only in the movies, though."

"What?"

Kelly said, "It's only the movies, though. Right?"

He didn't answer.

"Creeps, I don't think for her that this stuff is only movies. . . ."

"Don't call me Creeps."

"Sorry."

"Sheesh." Creeps stared high at the sun; it was threatening to peek out from behind the overcast. "Gwen doesn't; she never calls me Creeps. She calls me Kenny."

"Sorry."

His eyes definitely welled with tears now; he was embarrassed, hurting. "I love her. I . . ."

"What?"

"Nothing."

"*What?*"

136

He seemed to have taken a recent, sudden blow. "It's only movies, right?"

"What?"

"She wanted me to help her. Wanted me to help her play a game. It was only a game, like the movies we watched at her house."

"You went to her house to watch movies?"

"Why not?" Creeps backed away, defensive. "Why not? You used to go to Hanson's house all the time."

That was true. "And?"

"So she wanted us to play a game."

"A game?"

"With a gun."

Oh my God.

Creeps shivered, then said, "So I knew your mother was a cop, and I figured you guys would have a gun somewhere in the house. You did."

"We did? How would you . . ."

"I crawled in through one of your windows, looked around, and I found it."

This was incredible, and scary, the thought of Creeps crawling around inside of their house anytime he felt like doing it gave Kelly the shivers. *But what was Ms. Anders going to do with the gun? Why was Creeps crying now?*

Speaking very slowly, Kelly said, "Kenny, what's wrong?"

The sound of his proper name seemed to help. He said, "She . . ."

"She what?"

Sniffing, he said, "She wants me to kill her."

"What?"

"You heard me right, she wants me to kill her. Like in the movies. She loves me, and she wants me to kill her. Tomorrow night is Halloween, right? It's going to be our little trick-or-treat."

"Creeps, no . . ."

"It's what she wants. She wants to die. I guess it's what I want to—not her, but me. I want to die. Don't you, Kelly? Don't you ever want to die?"

"No."

"Don't you? At all?"

"No." Chilled by all of this, the fear Kelly felt of Ms. Anders was temporarily behind what she felt from Creeps.

"I don't know why," said Creeps. "Sometimes this life is so terrible. . . ."

Kelly reached for him, but Creeps jerked open his jacket, revealing the butt of the Beretta sticking out of his belt line. "It's almost Halloween, Kelly. The perfect time. You want to come with?"

Kelly froze. "No."

"Then stay away. Go play with your friends. I think your mother's calling."

Ma wasn't calling, but she wasn't home, either, so Kelly couldn't tell her about Creeps's having the gun. Not that it was going to make any difference in the general consensus that Kelly was losing her mind; so be it. She was beginning to suspect that perhaps she *was* losing it. One interesting thing, though; there was mail for Kelly when she got home that evening, which was unusual; usually when there was it was from Dad, or one of the other relatives. This was from *Impossible Detective* magazine. . . .

Ma didn't come home that night.

Terrific, Kelly thought as the hours slipped away. *I've got something to tell her—something to prove I'm not the loon they think I am—and she's caught up in something.* Except as the time dribbled on, Kelly began to grow more and more concerned.

No problem, she kept telling herself.

Nothing to be concerned with.

All she had to do was wait, be confident in her mother and the other officers, remember the pleasant thoughts, all of the police family briefings, and—

Forget that. She called the police station; not the public lines, the emergency and nonemergency, but the office line; the one that skipped the switchboard. Unfortunately, Detective Edgar answered, and Kelly felt almost nauseous talking to the creep.

"I'm trying to get hold of Detective Wozniak; is she around?"

"Kelly?"

Spare me. "Yes."

"How are you? Your mother's not around, she's

stuck out in the field. Might be a while.''

"She can't call?''

"Maybe not for a while. You want to leave a message for her? I'll stick it on her desk for when she checks out.''

Kelly said no, and hung up.

Then she brooded for another while, and decided to call the phone number in the letter that same night, while waiting for Ma to get home so she could get Creeps busted before the substitute talked him into doing anything terrible.

Should she have mentioned it to Edgar?

No way.

Kelly's only concern now was that Ma might not believe her about the murder-suicide thing, so she decided to leave that part out and just say that she saw him with the gun. The rest, she figured, would take care of itself; Creeps was bound to spill the beans.

But she needed to talk to Ma. It wouldn't be enough to talk to Detective Edgar, or Captain Morris, or any of the other police.

Standing in the kitchen, Kelly again unfolded the ad answer forwarded from *Impossible Detective* magazine and dialed the number; it was long-distance from Ohio. The letter was from a man who identified himself as a reporter who had been trying to track down Gwen Anders for a long time. Even after all of her suspicions, Kelly's heart almost popped on hearing this confirmation. "You know about her?''

"Oh, yes. I know all about her.''

"What is she?''

Not *who*, but *what*. There was a moment's silence on the other end before the man said, "Gwen Anders is something very different than what you're assuming, I think. Kelly, is it?"

"Yes."

"This isn't something we should really be talking about on the telephone; I need to come to Long Beach and maybe see you. I definitely want to see Gwen Anders."

"That might be difficult."

"Let's talk about that tomorrow, can we?"

Saturday, *Halloween*. Still, it wasn't as if Kelly had plans; unmasking Gwen Anders might make a nice little trick-or-treat surprise. "When are you going to get here?"

"I have to drive, so it'll probably take me until at least the early evening. How's seven o'clock?"

"At night?" That was awkward.

"Yeah, I've got a room reserved over at the Long Beach Holiday Inn already. As soon as I saw in the magazine she was holed up in Long Beach I figured on coming. Do you know where that is? Can you meet me there in the coffee shop? It's important we talk."

"I think so, too," said Kelly.

Saturday morning, Halloween. Outside it was cold, very cold, and Ma still wasn't home.

That wasn't unprecedented, but it didn't happen all that often, the all-nighters, and Kelly knew early on it wasn't that anything had happened to her. Doug the thug was home by ten and frying eggs, and he took a telephone call from Ma explaining what was what, but wouldn't pass the phone along

142

to Kelly. "She's busy, Knock-Knock," he said, dismissing her. "She'll be along in a couple more hours. I'm going to eat and get to bed."

Whatever. If for no other reason than to get out of the house for a while, Kelly went down to the mall, did a little necessary shopping, and then ran into the MoKid; her friend seemed embarrassed, and Kelly found out that was because she had a date.

Which was just a light enough thought to make Kelly feel better for a minute. "A date? Good for you—with who?"

MoKid lowered her eyes. "Brian Fredericks."

Bob and Janice, Tara and her boyfriend, now MoKid and Brian. Everybody was going to the Double J homecoming football game—Kelly had completely forgotten about that—and then to a couple of Halloween parties. Where did that leave Kelly, even assuming she cared. *Showing up with Tyrone?* That thought almost made her blush. *Spare me the aggravation*, she thought, although all of this weird stuff was soon to be over with. After that, who knew. . . .

MoKid seemed to seriously want Kelly along, although she could see how it might be awkward. Probably she just didn't want to endure a first date by herself. "If you want to stop by, we'll be at Ogre Nick's after the game, then out to the parties." Ogre Nick's was a burger place, fast food, a jukebox; lots of music and noise, especially on Friday and Saturday nights.

"Probably not," said Kelly, thinking that was

getting to be another one of the stories of her life. Probably not. . . .

Ma reacted immediately to Kelly's story about Creeps's having the gun, although that didn't necessarily mean she believed it. She picked up the telephone and dialed the station, and spoke to Edgar. "Phil? Patty. I need you to run a kid down for me . . ."

Ma explained the situation with the gun. "Newlan, first name Kenny," she said. "Goes to Double J, has classes with Kelly. A little bit off the deep end, very into bloody murder movies and he's got my gun. Put it out, but make sure everybody is real careful."

Ma hung up the phone and looked over to Kelly, who was putting her shoes on. "Where are you planning on going?"

"I've got to meet somebody tonight."

Ma shook her head. "Someone's coming to see us."

"What? Who?"

"Miss Kennedy; the counselor. She wants to talk to us all in our own environment; a family session."

No way. "A family session? You mean more of this counselling?"

"Yes."

"I did the counselling thing, Ma."

"We're all going to do it."

Even the thug? "What about Doug?"

"He will be. Not tonight, because he's working, but he'll be part of it."

"I don't need any of this, Ma."

"We all need it, Kelly."

"What time does it start? How long does it last?"

"Seven o'clock. Until nine I think." Ma disappeared down the hall to her room, and Kelly went upstairs to retrieve the letter again and make for the telephone. Not the greatest news. She attempted to call the reporter guy back, but there was no answer. He was probably already on the road, headed to Long Beach. *Damn.* All her friends thought she was a flake, they were going to be no help with something like this. So she worked up the courage to call Tyrone.

His mother brought him to the phone—he had a mother?—and Kelly said, "Listen, I need a favor."

"I'd like to do you a favor."

Kelly blushed. Even though she was on the telephone she blushed, and then explained to Tyrone what she needed him to do. He found it funny. "It's Saturday night, Halloween; what makes you think I don't have plans?"

"Do you?"

"Sort of, yeah."

"Sorry."

"Don't be sorry; I didn't say I wouldn't do it. So you need me to pick up this reporter at the Holiday Inn for you?"

"That's where he said he was going to be. At seven. I don't know what he looks like, but he'll be in the coffee shop waiting for me. Ask the waitress or something."

Tyrone was very amused. "Aren't you a little

young to be meeting guys at motels?''

"Tyrone, this is important. I need you to do this for me. Pick him up, and meet me somewhere around ten—I can be there by ten.''

"Where?''

"I don't know, where do you want to meet?''

Tyrone considered it a moment and finally said Pizza Hut. "If I'm going to be out playing chauffeur, I'm going to need to eat. Okay,'' he finally said. "I'll do this weird thing for you. But this means you owe me.''

That kind of surprised her. "Owe you what?''

"I don't know,'' he said, very slyly, very slowly. "I'll give it a lot of long, careful thought. And I'll see you tonight. . . .''

17

Tyrone never showed up at the Pizza Hut.

He promised, Kelly was fuming. He promised and he didn't come—the reporter guy was probably still at the Holiday Inn, if he hadn't blown the whole thing off as a joke already. She was burning angry when she stormed back outside of the restaurant, starting to head up the street when she was very nearly run down by a big red van sliding in close to the curb and honking; the horn had a funky warble, as if the battery was on the verge of dying, and for a chilling second Kelly thought she was being intentionally run down—*the substitute*.

But it was Tyrone.

The first thing Kelly saw when Tyrone slowed the van to pick her up was this: *he was excited.* Absolutely excited—or worked-up scared—and just the sight of any emotion on his face, that grinning leer, was enough to start Kelly's limbs quivering. "What is it?"

"Get in the van. Quick."

"What is it?"

"Get in—no, get in back. Hurry!"

Kelly hurried, pulled open the side door and

climbed in. Tyrone was away from the curb before she even got the door slammed shut; the guy in the passenger seat helped pull it tight. "Wait'll you hear," Tyrone said.

"What?"

"This guy can help you."

"Kelly, I'm Justin Jensen," said the man on the passenger seat. Grey-haired but not exactly old—early forties, late thirties—he had bushy eyebrows and wore sunglasses on despite the night. "We talked, but it's good to meet you. Everybody calls me J.J." He held out his hand.

"J.J.? Double J?"

"Yeah."

Kelly forced a laugh. "Our school is called Double J."

"I heard that."

Sniffing now, Kelly suppressed a grimace and the reporter noticed. "Sorry. This is my van; I apologize for the smell. That's the chemicals for the film stock; developing chemicals. I thought we could talk easier if I let your friend drive."

"I left my car at the Holiday Inn. I love driving vans," said Tyrone.

"Just be careful," said Kelly. "My ma's apt to have put an all-points bulletin out on me."

"Her mother's a cop," explained Tyrone.

That got the bushy eyebrows to rise. "Really? Well, that's good to know."

Kelly said, "You're a reporter?"

"Sort of, yeah."

"What do you mean, *sort of*?"

"Well, actually, I'm a producer for 'A Current Affair.' It's a television show."

"You are? Wow."

"Yeah, and what a TV news producer does is the actual reporting—the actual research, finding out the story so the on-air talent can recite the script with *my* film."

"You're the real reporter."

"Absolutely, and this thing with your substitute is bigger than you imagine."

"Yeah," said Tyrone, turning a corner, enjoying himself with the big vehicle. "Listen to this guy. I couldn't believe it myself."

"There's a big story behind Gwen Anders."

"I figured," said Kelly. "I know my own bad stuff about Gwen Anders."

"No," said Justin Jensen. "It goes way beyond what you think. Your sub is a very sick lady."

"I know."

"No, you don't know. Mostly it's not her fault. See, back in 1983 she was a celebrity. A special person."

"What do you mean special?"

"You ever heard of the Elmsboro Massacre?"

"No."

"I'm surprised. We did a big story on the tenth anniversary, you didn't see it?"

"No, I don't watch much TV."

"Elmsboro's a town in Illinois," explained the reporter. His bushy eyebrows scrunched in determination as he spoke. "Very small town, near the interstate highway. They've got a fast-food place there called Tango's, great food, but unfortunately

149

they also had a guy there called Oliver Passibe.
You've heard of him.''

''No.''

''Never heard of Oliver Passibe? I'm surprised,
he's a famous guy. Good old Ollie decided he was
going human hunting one day, and thanks to how
easy it is to buy machine guns in this country he
had lots of weaponry to hunt with.''

''Oh my God.'' Something was starting to come
back to Kelly, something she'd heard about this
long ago.

The bushy-eyebrowed reporter went on. ''There's
a statistic people almost never think about. Did you
know that most murders in America are committed
with handguns?''

''Yeah.''

''But did you also know that the weapon of
choice for your average serial killer is either a
sharp-edged knife, or his own hands—strangling,
ropes, that sort of stuff. One-shot killers go for
handguns, mass murderers prefer the personal
touch.''

Kelly shook her head; she didn't realize that.

''Except for our famous guy,'' said the bushy-
eyebrowed reporter. ''Except for Oliver Passibe.
He could never get the hang of knives, and simple
handguns just weren't enough for the results he was
looking for. Oliver Passibe hunted with a machine
gun.''

''No. . . .''

''Yeah. So Ollie strolls into Tango's at lunch-
time, and usually Tango's has at best four, six people there—this is a small town, they didn't even

have their own fire department, they had like two cops. But to make matters worse there's a school bus full of kids on a field trip inside—along with their teachers.''

The horrible thought struck immediately. ''Gwen Anders.''

''And two others. Actually, there was a bit of luck—the school trip was two buses, but one was delayed down the road with an overheated engine. Those were the kids who thought they were unlucky, missing lunch. But what they missed was Oliver Passibe and his machine guns. He killed thirty-one people—mostly kids—in what turned out to be America's worst day of mass murder in *history*.''

''Oh my God.''

''Ollie goes from table to table, shooting. He gets the kids who hid in the bathroom, the clerks and cooks behind the counter. The people who crawled under the tables, crying, begging; he shoots the wounded in the head with a .45 automatic pistol he carried.''

Kelly swallowed, feeling very sick.

''The only one he doesn't shoot in the whole place is Ms. Gwen Anders—no, Ollie grabs her out of a booth for execution, but then he stops and says something to her. And he leaves.''

Kelly felt her breath slip away. ''What did he say?''

''Nobody knows. All we know is he left her alive.''

''Left her?''

''Oh, yeah, that's the kicker. Oliver Passibe got

away. Got away in his pickup truck and drove it into the St. Joseph River and drowned—or so they say, they never found the body—but his last words on this earth were spoken to Ms. Gwen Anders. And she absolutely went out of her mind."

"I would too."

The reporter shrugged, as if he had never actually considered the question. "Like I said, Gwen Anders did go crazy—she got real self-destructive. Tried to kill herself, even had an affair with one of her students—all of her relationships started to border on the self-destructive. That would have got her fired—rumor was she was trying to convince the student to kill her, some sort of a sick murder-suicide pact—except the kid was in one of the big local families, and they couldn't have that come out."

"Murder-*suicide*?"

"Yeah."

Kelly exploded. *"That's what she wants to do with Creeps! What she wants him to do with her!"*

Justin Jensen accepted this grimly enough. "We need to see her. Now."

"That's where I'm going," said Tyrone.

That made Kelly nervous. "I don't know . . ."

The bushy-eyebrowed reporter was finishing up his story. "So the school system couldn't fire her, but they wanted to get rid of her. The town authorities felt bad about everything—how do you take these things out on a poor woman whose only sin was that she survived? Whose only crime was that a monster like Oliver Passibe sees something in her eyes so he spares her life?"

"I don't know."

"Nobody knows. But since they couldn't toss her in an asylum without drawing attention to what she'd done to go there, the town paid to have her relocated, have her past erased as much as possible. They didn't change her name, but they cut her ties. Even had her school and stuff start telling people who called that she was dead. Give the poor woman some peace."

"Except . . ."

"Except what?"

"Except I think Oliver Passibe is still alive, still out there. I think he might have seen our thing on TV about her, and if he saw your ad in *Impossible Detective*, he's probably on the way here."

"I did that."

Tyrone spoke up, saying, "That's what happens when you go running with a first impression—you don't trust people you should. Like *me*."

Kelly wasn't up for that now, all she could say, again, was, "I did that." She was the one who'd brought Passibe to town.

Another grim nod from the bushy-eyebrowed reporter. "Not realizing what you were doing, yes, I think you might have."

"Oh my God."

"This other stuff you mentioned on the phone, the calls, the letters to the substitute; I don't know what they might have done to her mind. God knows it was borderline breaking point as it was."

Kelly was reeling. "Oh, no . . ."

"The main thing is Passibe, though. If that lunatic somehow finds his way here . . ."

"He'd kill her."

"Maybe. Maybe she'll kill *him*; maybe this time she's the one who'll go on the murder spree." Jensen explained himself. "Remember, she's sick and self-destructive. God only knows what that monster said to her when he spared her life; I guess that's all she's been hearing at night all these years. Maybe she doesn't want to hear it anymore."

Kelly recognized the neighborhood they were in, but didn't place why they were there; the houses were farther apart, it was more rural. "And we're going to warn her?"

"I think that's the best plan. Tyrone said he knew where she lived."

"I've been there," said Tyrone. "Remember?"

Kelly did; she was glad she was sitting on a box in the back of the van, in the shadows. She was glad nobody could clearly see the look on her face; the guilt. Except it did stink back there. *Bad.* "Phew . . ."

The van was stopping and the bushy-eyebrowed reporter was agreeing again. "Sorry. Nothing smells worse than that stuff they develop videotape with."

Develop videotape? Kelly almost spoke up— *videotape didn't need to be developed. . . .*

"Is this the place?" asked the reporter.

"Yeah," nodded Tyrone. "That's her house. I was out here once—"

Slam! With one stretched hand, the reporter slapped Tyrone's face forward, into the steering wheel; there was a sickening crunch and the horn started warbling, loud and relentless; a groan from hell. Then he slipped and slid down onto the front seat. The horn stopped suddenly, but Tyrone wasn't moving, or making any sounds.

The reporter grunted and looked back at Kelly who had slammed herself back flat against the van wall in shock, her heart pounding. The reporter's bushy eyebrows didn't seem friendly anymore; they were arched, demonic. "Nope," he chuckled, lifting Tyrone by the hair and slamming his head against the steering wheel again. "Never could get the hang of knives."

Kelly made no sound; she couldn't, something was choking the wind from her guts. Maybe she got out a choke.

The bushy-eyebrowed guy spoke in horrible parody of Tyrone's words, saying, "And *that's* what happens when you trust people you shouldn't. Like *me*."

Kelly did choke now. "You—"

"Never, never liked knives or any of that stuff," said the bushy-eyebrowed guy as he let Tyrone fall again. He pushed his sunglasses up the ridge of his nose and grinned, saying, "But I am *still* a famous guy. . . ."

Then he was on her.

KIDNAPPED, ABDUCTED, VICTIM OF TERRORISM

IT COULD HAPPEN TO YOU!
A TOP PROFESSIONAL TELLS WHAT YOU NEED TO KNOW TO SURVIVE!

From cover of *Impossible Detective* magazine, November issue.

Kelly never read the article. . . .

18

What prompts madness?

Kelly felt the question throbbing through her brain as she awoke, surprised to be waking; surprised to be alive. *Isn't this amazing?* she thought, feeling herself breathe, in and out, in and out, whenever she wanted.

She was inside of a house; probably Ms. Anders's house. The lights were low; she was lying facedown on a thick carpet. She was in pain, she'd been attacked, but no permanent damage.

She wasn't bleeding.

She wasn't dead.

Oliver Passibe was nowhere to be seen.

But she could hear his voice. Rambling, midway through a nonstop monologue which unconsciousness had spared her—*perhaps*. Perhaps the parts she had been out for were now implanted in some special place in her subconscious, little time bombs ready to go off—

No! Ma, where are you? Doug—

Kelly stunned herself. The shocked small voice inside of her was even ready to cry out for Doug the thug.

Kelly tried to stand up, but her bad knee was on fire, screaming at her. She remembered the struggle now, in the van, how Passibe had kicked it out from under her before choking her with his hands until she passed out. She assumed he was killing, she was dying, but obviously he had something else in mind.

Where was Ms. Anders? Was she home? Away? Had Passibe already killed her?

Oliver Passibe reentered the room, continued rambling. "My apologies. Trick-or-treaters at the door, and I had to find some sort of a treat for them in an unfamiliar kitchen. Fortunately the substitute appears to enjoy a sort of a sweet tooth; the cupboards are full of candy."

"You . . . you gave out candy?"

"Certainly. It's Halloween; I'm not an old grump." Passibe paced around, talking. "I like Halloween, Christmas, holidays. You know, the problem with life, is that, except for holidays, life is little more than the Barmecide feast. Which you don't understand."

"No." Kelly tried to pull herself up, but she couldn't; the knee just would not function. Tears filled her eyes. *Come on. . . .*

Agony. The knee had popped apart as the doctor had explained to her one time; it was easily dislocated. It could pop right back on its own, but *that* pain would make this pain seem like *nothing*.

There was a big, heavy bookcase against the wall of the room, and Kelly crawled toward it as Passibe talked.

"The Barmecide feast," he said. "That's from

the tales of the Arabian Nights. It was a mammoth feast prepared by the prince for his beggar boy victim—only all the plates and bowls were empty; the servant girls brought jugs of wine with nothing in them. Sort of an analogy to life, don't you think?''

"I can't think.''

"Probably for the best.''

Almost to the bookcase, talking to distract Passibe. "Is Ms. Anders here? Did Creeps shoot her? Himself? Or did you . . .''

"No, Ms. Anders is not here,'' said Passibe, chuckling. "Isn't that just like life? You come such a long way to see somebody, and they aren't even home when you get there.''

"What about Creeps?''

Oliver Passibe shook his head in mock pity. "Listen to how cruel you sound, even now, Ms. Kelly. Even after you've supposedly become such a special, better person, calling another young man *Creeps* who did nothing more than offer you hope. If he'd just kept his mouth shut, you would never have been swept up in events totally beyond your control. You would never have seen any of this coming, would you?''

"I . . . I don't know.'' She reached up to the bottom shelf and pulled her weight up; the knee popped some and burned. *Would it slip back into place? How was she going to stand on it? How was she possibly going to run on it?*

"I don't know. *Well*,'' said Oliver Passibe, half-lost in a thought it seemed. "I guess such things depend on attitude.''

"I never understood . . .'' She started to say

159

Creeps, but corrected herself, saying, "Kenny. I never understood him." *What was she saying? Why did any of this matter? She needed to get out of there, forget all the theories and fantasies and worries*—this guy was a killer!

She pulled herself up by the third shelf.

Passibe strolled the living room. "Let's try looking at ourselves, Kelly; my understanding is you're so screwed up in the head you were living your life through your history teacher. Ms. Kelly Wallis, you were ready to live your life through a substitute history teacher."

"What?"

"Or so your boyfriend told me. While he was around."

"My what?"

"Our van driver."

Tyrone.

Kelly froze. She felt more than tense. *Humiliated.*

She tried another tactic. "You did that thing at that restaurant."

"Tango's. Oh, yes."

"What did you say? What did you say to Ms. Anders when you didn't shoot her? What made her so crazy?"

That amused Passibe. "So what would you like from me? Some great confession? I'm done confessing to you, Kelly; where does honesty get you? Why would you care about me?"

Kelly fought to stand up; *run away.* "I want to live."

"I don't believe that for a minute. You don't

want to live any more than Gwen Anders does. Or I do. But isn't resignation to fate such a *liberating* feeling?''

Tears were streaming down Kelly's face. ''*I do. I do want to live.*''

''Well. You want to know what I said to the substitute? I said—*why didn't you ask me to stop. I would have, you know; I would have stopped* shooting and gone somewhere else if only she had asked me nicely.''

Oh, God. . . .

''If only she had asked me nicely. . . .''

''You didn't mean it,'' said Kelly, struggling, breathing hard, in agony. ''You were just saying that to be cruel. You just left her alive to be cruel.''

''Ah, but you just said being left alive is never a cruel act.''

Kelly swallowed. Said nothing.

''It's an interesting question,'' said Passibe. ''Very interesting; maybe I'll try the equation again. Yeah. I saw this interesting burger place on my way into town—called Ogre Nick's; ever been there?''

Ogre Nick's—that was where MoKid and Bob and Janice and . . .

''You can't,'' said Kelly.

''I can. It'll give Ms. Gwen Anders a little more to think about, along with all the help you gave me.''

''No. . . .''

''Yeah, came prepared. Got my toys with me— what did you think was in the van? Besides the body of a nosy state trooper, I mean.''

Kelly involuntarily shuddered, nearly lost her balance, but she was just about up now, pulling herself up fifth shelf of the bookcase but Passibe's reaction was so quick, so casual, so casually *quick* that it was like a mongoose turning back on the snake. He didn't swing at Kelly, didn't shoot her, didn't throw a blow; he just pulled suddenly at the back of the bookcase and stepped aside.

Gravity did all the work.

"*Ahhhh!*" She screamed and the bookcase collapsed on Kelly, and the last thing she saw was a mountain of books raining down ahead of an oak wall which was falling. . . .

Smoke.

Kelly woke up to smoke, and pain. And darkness.

But she was alive. *Alive!* Her mind screamed the word, and she almost did it aloud, except she wasn't sure if Passibe was gone or not. What she could see was several small fires Passibe had set for her to expire in.

Trapped inside of the burning house, Kelly was pinned under the bookcase as the place filled with smoke and flames.

No! This wasn't right. Pushing against the weight of the bookcase, Kelly could taste anger and fear, fear and anger, as if together they were a lather which could neither be swallowed nor spit out. There was no way she was going to die this way, let him get away with this, let him get away with what he was going to do. Ogre Nick's! *No!*

Except . . . except she couldn't budge the thing,

162

and the room was hazy now, filling with sweet-smelling smoke. Coughing, Kelly covered her mouth and turned her head as low to the ground as she could—like they'd always taught in school—but this wasn't good. *Not good.*

The bookcase still wouldn't lift; the pressure only seemed to increase as she tried to push up and lift it. And the smoke was getting thicker, thicker, that stiff sulfur smell choking her; the drapes were on fire. The other room ablaze.

There was somebody standing over her.

Kelly reached out, *please....*

Tyrone?

No. He had a gun and was aiming it at her.

Oh, God. Kelly clenched her eyes shut, waiting for Passibe's bullet, but it didn't come. It wasn't Passibe.

It was Creeps.

Barely conscious when the oxygen mask was placed on her face, Kelly was carried over toward the ambulance. Fighting to wake, she scrunched and squinted and saw that the attending fireman was Doug the thug.

He didn't seem so much the thug now, though, working quickly to check the mask Kelly was coughing into. "Easy, easy," he said. "Just breathe it in and out, there's good oxygen there for you."

"*No.*" Kelly pulled at the mask, pulling it off of her face. She needed to talk, and she needed to be understood, was looking around. In one motion she rose, pushing Doug and his gear away and grabbing for her leg, standing, *pushing*—

Pop.

"*Ahhhhh!*" Kelly screamed; she couldn't help it. Doug and the ambulance guys were horrified, but Kelly could at least move her leg now; she collapsed back down on the gurney and called around. "Kenny! Kenny! Creeps!"

"Kelly, easy."

"*Kenny!*"

Creeps was there, approaching hesitantly, scared, embarrassed. No gun was visible now; it had been him who pulled Kelly out of the burning house, and he'd put the weapon away. "I thought you were Ms. Anders in there," he explained. "I saw the fire and thought you were ... without me, I mean ... I *thought* ..."

"Where's Gwen Anders? There's a killer out there! Oliver Passibe!"

"Who?"

Standing above Kelly, Doug was grim. "Another killer."

Kelly tried to lift herself off of the gurney, but Doug held her down and Creeps looked scared and confused. "He's going to Nick's! He's going to kill everybody there!"

Shaking his head, Doug said, "More killers. Listen, Kelly, you're lucky to be alive, and I think you've got an awful lot of problems. You didn't start that fire, did you?"

"We have to go to Ogre Nick's. Now! Call the police!"

"No, Kelly."

"Please." Kelly felt herself begging. "Please.

Doug, do this for me. Do this and I'll be on your side, I swear it.''

That shocked him. "I don't need anybody on my side.''

"Please.'' Kelly felt degraded, begging Doug like this; in a lot of ways it was worse than begging Passibe for her life, but it didn't matter, because she had to go, *now!*

Doug the thug eased back, pulling off his big helmet—LONG BEACH F.D. it said—and wiping at the sweat on his face. For whatever reason—guilt, maybe—he looked around once before shaking his head. "No way.''

Kelly made her final appeal, but it wasn't to Doug the thug, it was to Kenny Newlan; Creeps. "Help me. *Believe* me.''

Their eyes met and Creeps got the message, or maybe he didn't; maybe he made the decision on his own. Kenny Newlan pulled out her mother's gun. . . .

19

The gun got them the ambulance, and away from the burning house. Where it might get them next could not possibly be good. Kelly drove; Creeps didn't know how, but he got the siren working and that cleared the way. The vehicle flew, lights flashing all the way.

The radios in the ambulance were chattering; both the police scanner and the ambulance company's two-way.

"Central, two-four—stolen ambulance is en route to Ogre Nick's on Franklin. Copy?"

"Copy."

"Two-four disabled—can you get a pursuit?"

"How are you disabled two-four?"

"The punk shot one of my tires. Copy?"

Creeps looked over at Kelly and grinned. She didn't grin back, because the ambulance company chatter was relaying something from the fire department—they maintained direct lines with the ambulance companies. *"Number three, the fire department is responding to double alarm at Ogre Nick's on Franklin; do you copy?"*

"No . . ." Kelly banged a hand on the steering wheel.

The police radio said, *"Six-one, I have an alarm from Ogre Nick's on Franklin."*

"That's where those kids are going."

"I think we got a big problem there."

Kelly screamed now. "No!"

Except they got there too late.

There were no police yet, but as Kelly screeched the brakes the Ogre Nick's parking lot was in chaos, screams and panic and cars screeching in and out and more sirens were on the way, although Kelly wasn't sure if they were coming for her or whatever was happening here. Slamming open the ambulance door, she ran past some surprised people and started toward Nick's door before she and Creeps got stopped.

"No—wait," said a frightened-looking boy in an Ogre Nick's uniform. "You can't go in there, it's a hostage thing. There's a crazy guy in there."

The big Ogre Nick's sign was still shining, but the building lights were gone. Inside, there was a shot. Kelly jumped, but not as much as the boy in the uniform.

"It's not a hostage thing," said Kelly, steeling herself and forcing her knee to work despite the pain.

Agony. Her leg was on fire, but at least it worked now. Which, of course, didn't matter. Not anymore.

It was time to deal with it, all of it, everything she'd started since the first day the substitute Gwen Anders appeared in class. And there was no more room for optimism, either; no more bright sides.

This was the end of the world.

No longer an occasional doomsday. This was it.

Sirens were wailing, and Creeps offered Kelly the gun; she shook her head. "He doesn't want to be shot; he wants to be talked to."

She went inside Ogre Nick's.

Passing inside the double doors was like the act of death, the dying itself, because what she found in there was certainly something close to what hell would be like; it was a vision straight out of Dante's *Inferno*, or *Paradise Lost*, or some drunken preacher's nightmares. The scene was a fog; oily, silky smoke hung over everything. The power was gone, lights dashed, and only the glow of the emergency beacons illuminated the eating area. There were small fires burning back in the kitchen; grease fires. The sprinkler system had kicked on, dropping useless sprays of water and spreading the blaze. The weeping, wailing, and moans of the damned drowned the sounds of the flames and sprinklers.

And, worst of all, there was a devil.

Oliver Passibe was hunting humans.

Kelly expected to be shot immediately on entering—she really did, would almost have welcomed an end to the misery, but instead by entering saved a life. At least for the moment.

Passibe had a woman by the hair, and was holding his pistol to her head. Draped across his back, on a sling, was an Uzi machine gun. There was red on his hands—blood—and he snarled something inhuman as he seized the woman. He had already dealt with her companion; the body of a man in a Chicago Bears jacket lay sprawled, half-in, half-out of the booth. The woman was beyond begging, beyond sound, but when Passibe turned to stare at Kelly she did, too.

"Oliver, don't! Stop this!"

Passibe dropped his victim, who half crawled, half collapsed away as he strode, grinning, over toward Kelly. "Hey, the cripple girl," he said. "Have we paid a recent visit to Lourdes?"

"Sometimes I can get it to work again," said Kelly, amazed at how little she was trembling—at least on the outside. So she was her mother's daughter, after all.

"Well, my little fireproof Lazarus, have you come to watch?"

"You promised you'd stop."

"Ah, no, I apologize for the misunderstanding, but I said I'd stop if the right person asked me to, and she ain't here. But welcome to my party. Want a Coke? There's free refills."

What was she supposed to do now? Kelly wondered. *Jump the guy?* That would be madness; he had two different guns, and he was crazy, but she couldn't do nothing. Any second now he was going to resume killing—probably with her—and he was going to keep killing until he was out of victims, or until the police shot him.

Which they wouldn't. Not right away, Kelly realized in horror. They would assume it was a hostage crisis, and they would negotiate, they would talk, and Oliver Passibe would just keep popping.

Sirens. Lights. Lots of flashing lights which strobed through the big windows, casting colors on the smoke and fog. Ogre Nick's was becoming surrounded, which in her heart Kelly thought was bad.

No matter what happened, Passibe would never be persuaded he was going to repeat his disappearing act. He wasn't going anywhere this time; he was the guest of honor at hell's end of the world party.

"Oliver, I'm here."

Kelly looked, as did Passibe. There was a new guest at this end of the world party. It was the substitute, walking in and behind the haze of smoke and steam floating forward out of the burning kitchen area.

Ms. Gwen Anders, long blond hair shining like a beacon in the darkness, not clearly visible but striding now, around the blasted fast-food place as if it were a classroom; perhaps in her mind it was. She seemed lost, caught in more than one different world. "Everyone sit up, sit down. Form an opinion."

Passibe stared at her, fascinated. Kelly, the others, they were no longer of any interest to him. His attention was solely on the substitute.

Some of the trapped victims saw this as well; crawling, they were sneaking toward and out the side door and Passibe allowed them to go, the ones who had a chance. Kelly and another small group clustered around one of the back booths had no such opportunity; Passibe and the substitute were between them and the door.

Passibe watched Gwen Anders walk, not approaching, but speaking; her mind clearly shattered. By what? *By this*? Or—wondered Kelly—by me. The substitute said, "Pop quiz, get ready."

Passibe grinned. "You still haven't asked me to stop."

170

"Make up your own mind."

Passibe laughed.

Kelly screamed. "Tell him!"

"No tell, *ask*," said Passibe.

The substitute said nothing. Stepped forward from the smoke, and moved like lightning; no insane lethargy now, just *action*.

Except—Kelly saw this now—except it wasn't the substitute; it was Ma, and she fired six times into Oliver Passibe without hesitation. . . .

A SUBSTITUTE FOR MADNESS

From cover of *Impossible Detective* magazine, January issue.

Kelly never read this article either. . . .

20

Kelly ran into Creeps—*Kenny Newlan, Kenny Newlan, she kept telling herself that*—just a month or so later, in the waiting room at Dr. Kennedy's office. They crossed paths, him coming out, Kelly going in, although she still saw no point in it. Everybody else seemed to disagree.

Things had been bad, *sure*, but Kelly's world ended all the time, and she could still look on the bright side of things. The Ogre Nick's disaster had been nowhere near what it might have been. Three people died, sure, but one of them was Passibe, so he was gone, *forever*. Kelly and Creeps had gone from being criminals with a gun to heroes in moments; Ma was all over the papers again, with the story of how she had talked to the substitute that night, kept the lady under protective custody until Ogre Nick's exploded—and worn Gwen Anders's blond wig into the restaurant to end the situation.

Last time Ma got heralds for hesitation, something she swore she'd never do again. She hadn't. Bang-Bang Patty saved Knock-Knock Kelly and a whole lot of others.

Even Tyrone made it. Although badly injured, Tyrone had survived his attack; Passibe left him for dead on the substitute's lawn, but was wrong. He was strong and was going to make it, although he needed reconstructive surgery and his disposition was never going to be the same.

Maybe Tyrone needed a little time with Dr. Kennedy, thought Kelly. Maybe they could share their hours with the lady psychologist.

Creeps was the one who was really different; he was even dressing differently, the entire experience had turned him into a completely altered human being.

Unless it was an act, Kelly worried. Unless he was just going through the motions, pretending to be what everybody wanted him to be. Letting people use him all over again.

Who could tell?

As for what happened to Mrs. Hanson, Kelly was never going to believe it was suicide—*never*. No matter what Kelly's mother, friends, or psychologist tried to drill into her. Mrs. H had help making that move into the next world, and maybe it wasn't the substitute who did the helping, but somebody did, and Kelly's private mission in life now was to figure it out, track it down.

After all . . . there was always *Impossible Detective* magazine.

But it probably wasn't going to happen today.

The substitute was the one Kelly really felt sorry for, although she realized with every second's guilt that she was responsible for so much of dragging Gwen Anders down, breaking her, leading Oliver

Passibe to Long Beach. That was what Kelly and Dr. Kennedy spent a lot of time talking about: guilt, forgiveness, and the substitute.

"Gwen Anders will recover." Dr. Kennedy was sure of this. "She doesn't need to carry Passibe's crimes around in her head—they were his crimes, not hers. But I don't think she'll stay in Long Beach, either. Long Beach is another Elmsboro to her now, and she'll probably move on when she's dismissed from the hospital. Start again."

"Can I see her?" *Can I at least say I'm sorry?*

"I don't think that's a good idea."

Kelly shuddered. She'd destroyed so much.

"No," stressed Dr. Kennedy. "No. You're the one who has to work this all out as well. Long Beach isn't your Elmsboro, either, Kelly. You didn't do this. He did. *Passibe* did."

"Yeah," said Kelly, "but I'm the one who brought him to Long Beach. I'm the one who got him to Ogre Nick's. I'm the one who let him shoot the MoKid."

"No. She was just one of two very unlucky people, Kelly."

"Luck? You believe in luck?"

Dr. Kennedy didn't say anything. She hardly ever did, really, Kelly realized. Except it was true, and if there was one thing Kelly knew it was there was no getting around an end of the world. . . .

On the day before the day before Christmas, Kelly actually woke up feeling like a human being

175

again, as if the night's sleep had been a special, liberating experience. No nightmares, just the old thing, the pleasant anticipation feelings like when she was a little girl. Christmas was coming!

Oh, no, Kelly thought. She hadn't done any shopping!

Ma was more than happy to go down to LaPorte with her. Kelly could have gone to the mall with friends, which was all modern and efficient, but at Christmastime downtown LaPorte was more fun; it was old-fashioned, with holiday bells and holly hanging from the streetlamps, a Salvation Army band, bell-ringing Santas.

Besides, she wanted to talk to Ma, sort of let her know she was feeling so much better now. Doug the thug had been gone since before Thanksgiving, although Ma still saw him a couple of times a week. Supposedly he was the one in therapy. They'd offered Kelly counselling, but she wasn't ready for it; didn't feel she needed it.

It was Christmastime.

All Kelly wanted to do was enjoy it all, and maybe—finally—get a few minutes alone with her mother in a pleasant environment and explain herself. Which is what she tried as they walked down the sidewalk, sipping hot chocolate, enjoying the light snow flurry which danced around them outside of the Walgreen's. "See, it all started with Mrs. Hanson," Kelly explained. "Supposedly she killed herself, but I couldn't believe that. I still don't believe that. I figure Ms. Anders was so far bent from everything that happened to her, she didn't know what she was doing.''

Ma didn't say anything, merely sipped her hot chocolate.

Kelly swallowed, working up to it. "See, the thing about Mrs. Hanson—she would never have killed herself because her ex-husband got remarried. They still got along so well. Mrs. Hanson was a happy person, not depressed. She was always there when I needed her, always the person I could be with—"

"That's why I killed her," said Ma.

Kelly stared in shock. Say what?

"Who did she think she was, getting into my life, getting into our lives," said Ma, glaring now. "We didn't need her, Kelly. We didn't need that woman judging me, judging us."

"What?"

"I had to make her go away. I tried talking to her; that didn't work. She had you wrapped so tight. You're my daughter, not hers."

"Ma . . ."

"A person should know their place. Do you know what that made me look like, Kelly? All those personal family things you told her? Do you know what she must have thought, said about us?"

"She never said anything . . ."

"And she sure won't now."

Kelly just stared at her mother, realizing—realizing horrible things—the crushing news that the substitute wasn't the one who hung Mrs. Hanson in the closet, who covered up Sandy Hanson's murder. . . .

Tossing away her cup and zipping her jacket, Ma said, ''Come on, let's run down to Ames's Shoes. They've got a sale going. . . .''

⇛TERRIFYING TALES OF⇚ SPINE-TINGLING SUSPENSE

THE MAN WHO WAS POE   Avi
            71192-3/ $3.99 US/ $4.99 Can

DYING TO KNOW   Jeff Hammer
            76143-2/ $3.50 US/ $4.50 Can

NIGHT CRIES   Barbara Steiner
            76990-5/ $3.50 US/ $4.25 Can

CHAIN LETTER   Christopher Pike
            89968-X/ $3.99 US/ $4.99 Can

THE EXECUTIONER   Jay Bennett
            79160-9/ $3.99 US/ $4.99 Can

THE LAST LULLABY   Jesse Osburn
            77317-1/ $3.99 US/ $4.99 Can

THE DREAMSTALKER   Barbara Steiner
            76611-6/ $3.50 US/ $4.25 Can

SPINE-TINGLING SUSPENSE
FROM AVON FLARE

NICOLE DAVIDSON

THE STALKER	76645-0/ $3.50 US/ $4.50 Can
CRASH COURSE	75964-0/ $3.99 US/ $4.99 Can
WINTERKILL	75965-9/ $3.99 US/ $4.99 Can
DEMON'S BEACH	76644-2/ $3.50 US/ $4.25 Can
FAN MAIL	76995-6/ $3.50 US/ $4.50 Can
SURPRISE PARTY	76996-4/ $3.50 US/ $4.50 Can
NIGHT TERRORS	72243-7/ $3.99 US/ $4.99 Can

THE BAND
   by Carmen Adams   77328-7/ $3.99 US/ $4.99 Can

SHOW ME THE EVIDENCE
   by Alane Ferguson   70962-7/ $3.99 US/ $4.99 Can

EVIL IN THE ATTIC
   by Linda Piazza   77576-X/ $3.99 US/ $4.99 Can

RATS IN THE ATTIC AND OTHER STORIES
TO MAKE YOUR SKIN CRAWL
   by G.E. Stanley   77389-9/ $3.99 US/ $4.99 Can

Look for All the Unforgettable Stories by Newbery Honor Author

★ AVI ★

THE TRUE CONFESSIONS OF CHARLOTTE DOYLE
71475-2/ $3.99 US/ $4.99 Can

NOTHING BUT THE TRUTH   71907-X/ $4.50 US/ $6.50 Can

THE MAN WHO WAS POE   71192-3/ $3.99 US/ $4.99 Can

SOMETHING UPSTAIRS   70853-1/ $4.25 US/ $5.25 Can

PUNCH WITH JUDY   72253-4/ $3.99 US/ $4.99 Can

A PLACE CALLED UGLY   72423-5/ $3.99 US/ $4.99 Can

———————— *And Don't Miss* ————————

ROMEO AND JULIET TOGETHER (AND ALIVE!) AT LAST
70525-7/ $3.99 US/ $4.99 Can

S.O.R. LOSERS   69993-1/ $3.99 US / $4.99 Can

WINDCATCHER   71805-7/ $3.99 US/ $4.99 Can

BLUE HERON   72043-4 / $3.99 US/ $4.99 Can

"WHO WAS THAT MASKED MAN, ANYWAY?"
72113-9 / $3.99 US/ $4.99 Can